Blacklight

Also by Bill Knox

BLACKLIGHT

Bill Knox

Constable • London

First published in Great Britain 1967
This edition published in Great Britain by Constable,
an imprint of Constable & Robinson Ltd 2009

Copyright © Bill Knox 1967, 2009

The right of Bill Knox to be identified as the author
of this work has been asserted by him in accordance with the
Copyright, Designs & Patents Act 1988.

A copy of the British Library Cataloguing in Publication
Data is available from the British Library.

UK ISBN: 978-1-84529-916-3

Printed and bound in the EU

PEFC
PEFC/16-33-111
CATG-PEFC-052
www.pefc.org

Chapter One

Hungry but cautious, the young tope poised motion-less for an instant then flicked its tail, circled in a deceptively lazy style, and attacked. The needle-toothed, shark-like mouth swept on and closed with a snap into the soft, yielding lure – and next instant two feet of twisting fury exploded as the baited hook dug its barb deep and the nylon trace took the strain.

Maddened, the young tope lunged in a new direc-tion. A few feet away a strange, awkward bulk stirred on the sandy bottom, a bulk which rolled sluggishly as the fish exploded in fresh terror. But the nylon trace and its line were meant for much mightier challengers.

Half an hour later captive and silent, almost motionless captor were still linked by the fine, opaque thread. The long, dark length of a conger came near, considered what it saw, then, like others before it, sheered off in haste.

The man on the far end of the line had been dead for most of the night. The nylon had garrotted deep into his neck, the mark of its violence already almost buried in the swollen flesh. A single block of pig-iron ballast was roped around his middle.

It was daylight above before the tope stopped struggling, died, and the little sea-bottom creatures moved in.

* * *

H.M. fishery cruiser *Marlin* arrived in Loch Rachan at seven a.m. In the month of June on the West Highland coast of Scotland that meant the sun was already climbing into the sky – and the day ahead seemed set for fair. The sea was calm, only a wisp or two of cloud flecked the morning sky, and for once there seemed no immediate reason for the scowl which creased the face of her commander.

Captain Shannon, an elderly, bearded, moon-faced little man, stayed where he was on the bridge wing as *Marlin* slowed and her bow-wave died. Short, stumpy legs wide apart, he frowned out across the loch to where the village of Borland was still a sleepy cluster of cottages with smoke just beginning to rise from its chimneys.

Without turning, he nodded. Behind him Chief Officer Webb Carrick kept his face suitably expressionless and waved a brief signal towards the bow. The anchor rattled out, splashed, and bit bottom at four fathoms. As the chain tightened, Carrick winked briefly at the helmsman by his side then flicked the telegraph lever to 'stop engines'.

Marlin's powerful twin diesels purred for a moment longer then died, leaving only the hum of her generator plant and the soft lapping of the sea against her hull. The Blue Ensign of the Fishery Protection squadron fluttered lightly at her stern and the escort of gulls she'd acquired at first light hovered patiently overhead.

'Join me for breakfast, Mr Carrick.' From Shannon, it was no invitation but a command. 'Tell the bo'sun I want a boat within the hour. We'll probably have visitors when I get back. Tell him that too.' The small, almost squat figure didn't wait for an answer but brushed past and stumped down the companionway ladder in the direction of his cabin.

Carrick sighed ruefully, lit a cigarette, tossed another towards the helmsman, then reached for the bridge telephone and pressed one of the panel buttons. The intercom buzz ended with a click and an answering grunt.

'Bridge,' said Carrick briefly. 'Clapper, the Old Man's going ashore in about an hour. He'll probably be bringing back company. Make sure we're presentable.'

There was a short silence as Petty Officer William 'Clapper' Bell, *Marlin*'s bo'sun, digested the information. Then his voice rumbled.

'Ach, now look, sir –'

'I know,' soothed Carrick. 'You've got troubles. But either paint them or hide them – keep the taxpayers happy about how their money is spent.'

He hung up, and looked out across the bay.

Marlin lay about a quarter mile from the shore, almost opposite Borland village. Little different from a score of other inlets on the same lonely coastline, Loch Rachan was a two-mile finger of blue water and shingle beach edged by raw grey rock and rising, gorse-covered hills. An occasional cottage, low-walled and whitewashed, formed its own landmark on the otherwise empty slopes.

Borland village, small and neat, would normally have fitted the rest of the tranquil picture. But for the moment that had changed. More than a score of small craft jostled at moorings around the single frail wooden jetty, ranging from chunky cabin cruisers to open-decked launches, a couple of fishing drifters and a big old sailing ketch.

They formed the reason why *Marlin* had called at Loch Rachan, a place not normally on her schedule. Called, too, on her first patrol after a month in harbour with her crew on leave and a squad of dockside workers busy on the annual refit – a refit which had

7

left Clapper Bell swearing that it would be at least another month before he had things ship-shape.

The newly created Loch Rachan deep-sea angling championship, euphemistically described by its promoters as the Festival of the Western Seaways, seemed to have attracted a reasonable entry, and those same promoters had had the bright idea of asking for a courtesy guard ship as a sign of official approval. *Marlin*'s arrival was the last-minute reply. Carrick shrugged. If it kept them happy and meant a day or two's break from normal routine he'd have few complaints.

'Sir . . .' The helmsman, a long-faced east coaster named Harrison, cleared his throat with delicate care and waited hopefully. They'd been under way all through the night from the squadron base at Greenock, including an extra, fruitless sweep north after a report of a foreign trawler doing a spot of illegal netting well within the limits. He'd been on duty watch since two a.m., and his head still throbbed like a steam-hammer at the thought of the last session of drinking time he'd spent ashore before they sailed.

'Find some breakfast then get your head down,' agreed Carrick. A slight smile touched his lips. 'And Harrison –'

'Sir?' The helmsman eyed him warily.

'Next time take more water with it or you could be in trouble.' There was a lazy emphasis behind the words which made their meaning clear. Carrick took a last glance across the water to where the first few figures were appearing aboard the angling fleet, tossed his half-smoked cigarette over the side, and headed below.

Breakfast with Captain Shannon involved a certain minimum standard of protocol, starting with a wash and a shave. Once he'd reached his own small, 'tween decks cabin aft, Carrick peeled off his uniform jacket and the white roll-neck sweater he wore beneath, kicked out of his thick-soled seaboots, and padded over to the washbasin.

He was splashing vigorously when the cabin door clicked open.

'Welcome to bustling Loch Rachan, hub of the ocean lifelines,' declared a familiar voice with an air of mock enthusiasm. 'As for night life – heck, sometimes the deer come down from the hills!'

Carrick groped for a towel, wiped, turned, and grinned. Jumbo Wills, *Marlin*'s young second mate, owed his nickname to his build, and at that moment wore overalls and an ancient, dirtied shirt.

'Just where do you think you're going in that rig?'

Wills shrugged. 'There's some crawling around the forepeak to be done, skipper's orders – the kind of dirty job delegated to the underprivileged like me. Once I've had some breakfast anyway. Coming?'

'I'm summoned to the Old Man's table.' Carrick dried the rest of his face then tossed the towel aside. 'And he won't be happy to find you wandering around like something out of the bilges. He's expecting company later on.'

The younger man flushed to the roots of his fair hair. 'But if I don't get the forepeak organized he'll blow a gasket!' Jumbo Wills had two main fears in life – being seasick, which happened at least once a patrol, and running foul of Shannon which happened even more regularly. 'Unless I get straight to it and skip breakfast –'

'Why not?' Carrick found his electric razor, winked, and tried to soften the blow. 'Anyway, it might be worth while. Maybe he'll bring back some of the visiting talent.'

'Girls?' Wills brightened briefly then shook his head. 'No, not at an angling shindig. Anything female will be around fifty and wearing a moustache – I know the type.' He was still curious, however. 'Any idea why the Old Man wants you along? There's bound to be a reason.'

'But he hasn't told me yet.' An angry thumping on the opposite bulkhead made Carrick wince and lower his voice. The next cabin was occupied by Pettigrew, the third mate. Oldest of the trio, Pettigrew spent most of his off-watch time in his bunk and hated being wakened. 'I'll let you know what happens.'

'Well, I'll get on with it.' Jumbo Wills rubbed one hand down the greasy front of his overalls, sighed for his lost breakfast, and ambled out.

Carrick pushed the door shut behind him, set the razor buzzing, and began shaving. The face that looked out at him from the mirror had changed a little in the two years he'd spent with Shannon on *Marlin*. Perhaps – though he was barely conscious of the fact – it had become more weather-bronzed and had gathered a few extra lines of experience around the eyes.

His earlier, deep-sea time seemed like another, almost cosseted life. That chapter had ended when, a newly won master's ticket in his pocket but no ship available, he'd suddenly been called for a Fishery Department interview on the strength of a long forgotten application. The interview had finished with his being appointed Chief Officer under Shannon and being handed the black warrant card which made one Webster Carrick an assistant Superintendent of Fisheries. The job, in simple terms, amounted to being a combination of sea-going policeman and Civil Servant, with the disadvantages of both.

He grimaced at his reflection in the mirror while the razor buzzed on. Thirty-one years old, a stocky five foot ten in height, Carrick had a face which was broad-boned with lips a little too thin to allow any idea that his easy-going manner meant he could be pushed around. The rest was dark brown eyes and darker brown hair, muscular shoulders and, as he'd admit, a faintly cynical outlook on life.

Still, he liked that life. He switched off the razor and began to whistle while he packed it away. The tune was still shaping when the thumping renewed from Pettigrew's side of the bulkhead. Carrick shrugged a silent apology and hummed under his breath while he pulled on sweater and jacket once more and slipped his feet into shoes. He was ready for Shannon, whatever that ruddy-hued individual might have in mind.

Captain Shannon's day cabin was immediately below *Marlin*'s bridge. It was moderately large and first-time visitors were surprised by the bright chintz curtains at the portholes, curtains which his wife renewed as her personal contribution to each annual refit. But otherwise it was an accurate reflection of Shannon's outlook – sternly practical from spotless white paintwork to the gleaming brass of the roll pendulum and repeater compass hanging above his leather-topped desk. A bookcase held a much-used collection of Fishery Department handbooks, the furnishings were plain but comfortable, and frivolous decoration was restricted to an old lithograph of a sailing ship, picked up as a bargain at an auction sale.

When Carrick knocked and entered the table was already set for two and a coffee pot steaming to one side. Shannon had changed into his best shore-going rig, and was standing by the desk, an almost empty whisky glass in hand. He nodded a greeting while the ship's white-coated steward materialized in the doorway, brought in two plates of bacon and eggs, then left them as silently as he'd come.

11

'Good.' Shannon drained the last of the glass and gestured Carrick towards one of the chairs. 'Let's eat, mister – and I want to hear what state you reckon we're in.'

Refits always worried Shannon, who trusted no one when it came to matters affecting *Marlin*'s efficiency. Perhaps with good reason – like the rest of the flotilla of protection cruisers she had to cover an average of 17,000 sea miles a year on her beat from the Butt of Lewis in the north down to the southern limits of the Solway. It was a coast which rated among the most treacherous in the world, where a smooth-running ship was the best insurance against disaster.

Despite her role, no guns broke the line of *Marlin*'s distinctive grey silhouette of high-raked bow and squat single funnel. Her authority was the thirty knot speed of her twin 2,000 h.p. diesels, the Blue Ensign with the gold Fishery badge which flew at her square-cut stern, and Shannon – particularly Shannon, who rated as a Superintendent of Fisheries with the power to be his own judge and jury in most fishing disputes.

Breakfast stretched out while Carrick talked and Shannon questioned, then at last, satisfied, the older man fell silent. Carrick watched while Shannon poured himself a third cup of coffee, studying the bearded figure, vaguely amused at the aggressive way in which he tackled even the minor chore of adding sugar. *Marlin*'s skipper had a job to do, his ship was his particular instrument – four hundred tons and one hundred and eighty feet of go-anywhere power built like a miniature destroyer, manned by a crew of twenty and three watch-keeping officers. And the job? Keeping the peace and maintaining the law in the multi-million pound Scottish fishing industry, where life could be dangerously harsh and tempers boisterously quick.

Fishermen were supposed to know the rules which governed so many things from permitted nets and gear to seasonal bans and such basics as three-mile and six-mile operation limits. But fishermen had their own essentials – get the fish, get the market, get the money. Sometimes they'd claim breaking or bending the Fishery Department rules meant the only way they could pay the grocery bills.

Shannon, like the other protection cruiser skippers, had to beat them at their own game when it came to the tricks of the fishing grounds. But he was over sixty now, with only a few years left before he'd be compulsorily retired to draw a civil service pension and, if there was one to spare, have some minor medal pinned on his chest.

An impatient snort jerked him back to the present.

'I said, Mr Carrick, that if anyone thinks this guard-ship routine is an excuse for loafing they're wrong.' The sharp eyes opposite glinted balefully. 'This is Tuesday, their competition starts tomorrow and lasts till Friday, and officially we'll be around all the time. But that doesn't mean we'll be resting on our backsides. We weren't sent here just to brighten the lives of some rod-and-line enthusiasts trying to win silver cups for their sideboards.' Shannon rose abruptly from his chair and paced across the cabin towards his desk. 'Come over here.'

Puzzled, Carrick obeyed. Shannon pulled a rolled-up chart from the collection on a shelf, spread it carefully on his desk, and beckoned Carrick closer. One stubby finger swooped down to tap the printed sheet.

'Here's Loch Rachan, on the mainland. Out there –' his finger shaded west a little – 'we've got the Sound of Jura. On the other side are the islands, Jura, Islay, all the rest. Between the mainland and the islands there's plenty of deep water, correct?'

Carrick nodded. Once clear of the coastal fringe of rocks and minor islets a ship could have a hundred fathoms and more under her keel ... though there were dangerous exceptions to that rule.

'Right.' Shannon looked up from the chart. 'Read Admiralty memos as you're supposed to and you'll know they've established a new area of water south of Kilberry Head as a submarine exercise area. This section –' his finger traced a long oval on the chart. 'Usual notices to fishermen were posted at all ports.'

'And they didn't like it,' mused Carrick. 'There was some talk of a petition –'

'They seldom like anything,' said Shannon sourly. 'The Navy have gone ahead with the usual drill – warnings of exercise programmes, dates and times, a ban on fishing in the area when exercises are in progress. You may not have noticed it, mister, but we had a periscope stalking us for a good half-hour this morning when we came through the Sound.'

Carrick cleared his throat hastily. 'Anything special about this exercise programme, sir?' Usually the main NATO submarine training went on around the Kilbrannan deep, round in the Firth of Clyde – conventional submarines, sometimes a British or American nuclear unit thrown in. The British base at Gareloch and the American Polaris depot at Holy Loch were both close at hand. But the Navy liked to expand into new areas from time to time.

'Mostly the usual – diving practice, periscope stalks, practice torpedo shoots.' A thin wisp of humour entered Shannon's voice. 'You know the drill on the torpedo shoots, mister. The real thing but fitted with a dummy warhead – and a tender handy to collect it at the end of its run. At least, that's how it should go. Sometimes they lose one.'

It shouldn't happen, but it did. Carrick had seen the practice 'fish' often enough at the Gareloch Flotilla base. Their warheads were painted bright orange, with a built-in light and a self-igniting smokepot as other aids to their recovery. At the end of their firing run a compressed gas cylinder blew the liquid ballast out of the dummy warhead, and in theory the torpedo then popped up and floated around waiting to be reclaimed. But things could go wrong, a torpedo's gas cylinder fail to work, the nose become stuck in bottom silt.

The Navy didn't like losing a torpedo that way. In hard cash each 'fish' represented some three thousand pounds, with some of the newer types costing maybe three times that amount to replace. They'd search – but often the hunt only ended when a trawler or a drifter found an unexpected catch in its newly torn nets. That could be the starting point of a battle between a compensation-conscious skipper and some Admiralty department tied to a miserly reward system.

The hint of amusement in Shannon's voice caught his interest.

'They've lost one recently?'

Shannon nodded. 'Three days ago, a few miles south of here, near Whip Lighthouse. An experimental model of some kind, with a bigger than usual fuss about trying to find it again. That's their problem. Ours is these exercises are still going on, in the same area – and it happens to fringe on some of the best fishing marks in the whole Sound of Jura.'

'So we've to do a traffic cop act and make sure our anglers don't go wandering into the middle of a war game?' The smile wiped from Carrick's face. Chasing commercial fishers out of a prohibited area was one thing. But trying to control a scatter of wandering amateurs sounded ten times worse.

'They've been warned.' Shannon let the chart roll shut, snapped a rubber band round it, and put it back

15

in place. 'But there's a "champion angler" title and a ruddy silver cup waiting the man who lands the heaviest catch over the next three days – not to mention another for the best fish. Some might be tempted to sneak south and try their luck there. Particularly if they've hired a boat with a skipper who's hoping for a bonus if his man wins this dam' fool festival.'

'They might catch more than they expected,' murmured Carrick. 'Any prize for hooking and gaffing a sub, sir?'

Shannon grunted with little humour. 'It's more likely to be the other way round – some angler end up with a torpedo up his stern. Even a dummy warhead packs a wallop.' He glanced at his watch and scowled. 'I'm due to go over to the village and make polite noises to the festival organizers. I want you to follow after a spell on some excuse or other, look around the boats and find out what the skippers have in mind. Let them know we're not looking for trouble, but that we won't take kindly to strays.'

'I see.' Carrick walked slowly to the porthole and looked out across the bay. The sunlit water seemed drenched in blue, embroidered near the shore with fine white wavelets. 'Thinking of any boats in particular, sir?'

'These drifters, for a start.' Shannon lifted his gold-braided hat from the hook behind the cabin door and rammed it squarely on his head. 'I don't know much about the *Blue Vine*, but the *Anna B.* is one the Department has had trouble with before. Keep an eye on them both – and on the rest.' He opened the door and drew a deep breath. 'I can think of more important things *Marlin* could be doing, than playing nursemaid to the Navy, Mr Carrick. But if their exercises are fouled up Admiralty will chew Department, Department will chew me – and I'll do some chewing on my own!'

16

Carrick followed him up to the main deck, waited until Shannon had boarded the launch alongside, then watched as it drew away, heading towards the jetty. He turned away, lit a cigarette, then walked slowly towards the stern. A hoarse voice reached his ears, telling a couple of deckhands their possible fate if they didn't put more energy into stretching a new canvas over the davit-mounted whaleboat.

Carrick reached the scene, stopped, listened, and interrupted mildly. 'Bo'sun –'

'Sir?' Petty Officer Bell, six feet of bulky, ginger-haired Glasgow Irishman, looked round and grinned. 'Just makin' sure we're organized like you asked.'

'So I heard,' agreed Carrick dryly. 'Everything all right?'

'Aye, or it will be,' nodded Clapper Bell deter-minedly. 'As long as nobody pokes his nose into the wrong corners.' He glanced back at the toiling sea-men. 'Tighter, Hamilton – that's not your mother's apron strings you're tuggin'.'

The bo'sun's background was Royal Navy, with a string of faded medal ribbons on the breast of his money jacket to prove it. If he said things would be all right then that was exactly what he meant.

'Captain Shannon wants me to circulate among the competition boats and talk to some of the crews,' Carrick told him. 'Like to come along?'

'Nothin' better,' declared Clapper Bell enthusiast-ically. 'Eh, any chance of . . .' He left the rest unsaid, but bent one elbow a significant fraction.

'At this hour of the morning?' Carrick was more than doubtful. 'The local bar won't be open yet.'

'Och, they'll have bent the rules a bit for the fest-ival,' said Bell optimistically. 'And there's no better place to find out what's happening, provided a man has a glass in his hand to avoid lookin' conspicuous.'

Carrick shoved his hat further back on his forehead, sighed, and gave in. 'All right. Be ready in five minutes – we'll take the packboat. Your job is to get the locals talking on what the fishing's been like lately.'

'Aye, that was on my mind,' nodded the bo'sun in solemn approval. 'Eh . . . do I mention this torpedo that's gone an' wandered?'

Carrick grinned and shook his head. However he did it, Clapper Bell had a personal grapevine which seemed to stretch all the way to the Admiralty and back.

A few of the angling boats were already putting out when Carrick climbed down into the rubber packboat. Clapper Bell steadied it against *Marlin*'s side and shoved them clear as Carrick yanked the starter cord. The forty h.p. outboard howled briskly to life, then as the throttle eased back, its note steadied to a throb.

'I thought this fishin' lark didn't start till tomorrow,' frowned Bell, draping his bulky shape into a more comfortable position as they headed for the jetty. An old motor cruiser passed by, on its way to the open sea, a handful of equipment-festooned anglers gathered by its stern.

'Most of them'll be putting in some practice time,' said Carrick briefly. 'Then they'll spend the rest of the day arguing about just what tackle to use for the real thing.'

'An' none of them sayin' what they really think so that they've a better chance than the other fellas?' Clapper Bell chuckled, shifted round, then raised a startled eyebrow. 'Hey –'

Carrick had already seen what worried him.

The big drifter had been edging her way clear of the rest of the cluster of boats and now was really under way, diesel exhaust thundering from her stove-pipe stack, a busy white wake churning from her stern . . . churning while she swung in a curving course which was bringing her straight towards the packboat. It was the *Anna B.* As she drew closer he could see the blob-like faces of passengers on her deck and, behind the wheelhouse glass, the motionless figure of the man at her helm.

Clapper Bell growled, rose in a half-crouch, and waved his arms in irate protest.

The *Anna B.* kept on coming, as if drawn by a magnet. Carrick swung the tiller in a tight turn to starboard to clear her path, and as the rubber boat started to swing the drifter's bow came round to match.

'The daft basket –' Bell looked towards Carrick, saw the matching anger in his narrowed eyes, and fell silent. The packboat's engine bellowed at full throttle, they shot forward – and next moment the drifter was going past their stern, travelling like a train, close enough for them to count the individual rivets on her black, age-worn hull. There was open-mouthed surprise on her passengers' faces, but the man at her wheel leaned out, grinned, and spat briefly over the side.

Clapper Bell swore bitterly as the packboat tossed wildly in the *Anna B.*'s turbulent wash, then glared after the drifter's diminishing shape.

'What the hell was that all about?' he demanded.

'Someone feeling frisky,' said Carrick softly. He was storing away the memory of that face behind the wheel – grinning, unshaven, with unusually high cheekbones and close-clipped, greying hair. When he met up with that face again there would be trouble in store.

Another, smaller, craft came creeping out and passed without fuss. He relaxed a little, and noticed Bell peering intently over the side. There was maybe twenty feet of water beneath them, the bottom a patchy mixture of rock, fine sand and the occasional, isolated patch of waving green weed.

'Not bad down there,' mused Bell. 'Eh – I could use a chance later to check those new regulator valves, sir.'

Carrick nodded. The conditions were ideal for some not too serious aqualung work. As *Marlin*'s skin-diving team, he and the bo'sun made a particular point of carrying out their own checks and maintenance on the scuba gear. They'd both learned long ago that few things made a man more careful than the knowledge that his own safety depended on the attention he gave to otherwise humdrum tasks.

'Later on,' he agreed. 'I'll square it with the Old Man first.'

They threaded through the first of the moored craft, reached the jetty, and bumped gently against one of its wooden piers. Clapper Bell hopped ashore, looked around him, and beamed.

'I'll stay with the boat for a spell,' Carrick told him. 'But don't stray too far.' He gave a brief wave, opened the throttle a notch, and eased the packboat away at a gentle purr. The sun was warm on his face as he steered out towards the first target on his list, the *Blue Vine*.

Bigger and newer than the *Anna B.*, her gear spotlessly clean, the *Blue Vine* was still typical of most of her kind – about fifty feet long, with a little wheelhouse aft, fish hatches, winch and a derrick boom for'ard, carefully stowed nets along her deck. Her register number was painted in large white letters near the bow, and just above that her name stood proud in fresh gold lettering.

A group of men in holiday-style sports shirts and slacks were systematically chopping bait into pails near the derrick. They looked up for a moment as the packboat approached then returned to their task, but a deckhand lounging by the wheelhouse reacted differently. He slipped from sight down a small companionway and a moment later another figure appeared on deck. Tall and thin, a woollen stocking-cap on his head, wearing a grey flannel shirt and what looked like ex-Navy bell-bottoms held at the waist by a heavy leather belt, he nodded a greeting which was part invitation.

Carrick tossed him the packboat's painter, waited until the fisherman had given it a half-turn round the nearest deck-rail, then swung himself aboard.

"Morning.'

'And a good one.' A pair of keen grey eyes in a calm, leather-tanned face inspected him with mild curiosity. 'From *Marlin*, eh?'

He nodded. 'Just looking around – the captain thought that if we had to be guard-ship we'd better know something about what was likely to happen.'

'That sounds like old Shannon.' There was a faint amusement in the slow, north-east accent. 'The name's Jenkins Batford – skipper and part-owner.'

Carrick completed his side of the introductions, then looked around with casual interest. A few more pails of bait, mostly small mackerel, were lined up at the stern beside a carefully lashed collection of dhan-buoy markers, each topped with a small yellow pennant. The deck was still drying after some recent hose-cleaning, and the sunlight glinted on the wheel-house brasswork. Jenkins Batford ran what Clapper Bell would have called 'a real tiddly ship'.

'There's a mug o' tea to spare if you've time,' invited Batford. 'Want to come down?'

'Thanks.' Carrick followed him to the short companionway ladder, ducked his head to avoid the hatch cover as they descended, and found himself in the *Blue Vine*'s cramped little galley. The deckhand he'd seen earlier looked up in surprise from his seat at the centre table, and glanced at Batford.

21

'Better go up, Danny,' nodded Batford. 'Let me know if our man shows up – though we're not waitin' all that much longer.'

Danny nodded, shifted the cigarette in his mouth, and squeezed past them on his way to the deck.

'I'm taking eight o' them out,' explained Batford for Carrick's benefit. 'Six pounds a head per day –'

'And bonuses?'

'Depends on what luck the Almighty sends them.' The *Blue Vine*'s skipper seemed reasonably hopeful. 'But if I can give a little help to the process then I'd call it good business. The basic money's good enough, an' it makes a bit o' a break from the usual.' He walked over to the galley stove, unhooked a massive brown teapot, found a couple of mugs, and poured two measures of tarry brew.

'Sugar an' milk over in the corner,' he invited, passing one to Carrick.

'Right.' Carrick helped himself. 'Planning to work any special marks?'

'A few.' Batford sipped his mug and eyed his visitor quizzically. 'Places I know. Skinner Jones on the *Anna B.* has probably a few ideas o' his own too. You – ah – saw him, eh?'

'That's one way of putting it.'

'Aye.' Batford's sympathy was difficult to place. 'It's just that Skinner doesn't like Fishery men. Another of your cruisers, *Skua*, I think it was, caught him usin' a prawn net out o' season in the Minch last year – twice in a fortnight. The fines brought him close to bursting a gut, an' the four layabouts he's got for crew felt pretty much the same.' He hitched his free thumb into the leather belt at his waist. 'Still, that's not why you're here, is it?'

'No,' agreed Carrick. 'Let's say I'm making sure the word is passed we don't want boats straying into the Navy's exercise area.'

Batford took it calmly. 'I've no need to go there, Mr Carrick. What I've got in mind is different, very different. If I'm lucky, these rod an' line men I'm carrying might hit a tunny or two.' He sensed Carrick's unspoken doubt and smiled a little. 'You've got to know where to go, but there's the occasional run of them in these parts, an' a few other warm-water fish the experts don't expect – blue shark and porbeagle, some really big tope. Something to do wi' the Gulf Stream, a marine biologist once told me. Outside of that, well, their best hope is the skate, maybe cod, or wreck-fishing for conger.'

Tunny was real big-game fishing. But hitting a two hundred pound skate could be an equal experience – and the big conger eels, hugging their shelter, might give any angler a fight to remember. Carrick nodded, then looked round as feet clattered on the companionway ladder.

The newcomer who appeared stopped halfway down the rungs, glanced in his direction, and raised an eyebrow. He was a young man with long dark hair, blue denims, and a black leather jacket worn over a grimy string vest.

'A visitor from *Marlin*, Davey,' explained Batford. 'Mr Carrick, this is Davey Gwynne, our engineer. Sorted things out, lad?'

Gwynne nodded. 'She'll do. When do we leave?'

'When our Mr Broom shows up.' The *Blue Vine*'s skipper rubbed the smooth surface of the mug against his chin. 'Better tell those others it's not our fault.' As the engineer grunted and clambered up again, Batford thumbed towards the old alarm clock hanging from a nail on the bulkhead opposite. 'Be ready to sail at eight, they say – and as they're paying the bill we're happy to oblige. But don't ask me where this Broom has gone – probably he's still in his bed at the hotel.'

'Going to wait much longer?'

'No.' Batford glanced at the clock again. 'Another ten minutes then off we go. Davey had a wee spot of bother wi' one o' the fuel injectors, so we could use the time till now. But if these anglers are to get a hook into anything worth while this morning we'll have to sail, one short or not.' He cleared his throat significantly. 'Now, anything else, Mr Carrick?'

'Not for now.' Carrick drained the last of the tea, set the mug down, and turned towards the ladder. 'Well, good fishing, skipper.'

'Fishing?' Jenkins Batford shook his head. 'I wouldn't call this pole an' string stuff fishing, Mr Carrick. Not proper fishing at all.'

Carrick chuckled, and left him still shaking his head. On deck, the *Blue Vine*'s passengers were gathered in an impatient huddle round her engineer. They paid no attention as Carrick dropped down into the packboat, loosened the painter, and headed on his way.

More of the angling fleet had headed out. Others were getting ready to leave. He edged alongside a couple of small lobster boats, spoke to their skippers in turn, then was hailed by a tweedy, elderly man in an open fifteen-footer – a 'lone wolf' entrant who wanted to know when next high tide was due. The craft at the next mooring was an old converted lifeboat, manned by a family with a tribe of small, noisy children. Next in line, the big sailing ketch was silent and deserted, but as he rounded its stern, heading in for the jetty, he saw something which drew a soft whistle of admiration to his lips.

The name on the sleek-lined bow was *Starglow* – and the cream-painted motor launch, with a full-width cockpit bridge, a slim, angled stern and twin bronze screws glinting beneath the water, looked as if she'd amount to a sizeable portion of anyone's bankroll. Two long fibre-glass poles branched like

24

antennae from fishing chairs mounted one on either side near her stern.

Carrick brought the packboat nearer. The cockpit bridge was empty, but one of its doors lay half-open, moving gently with the motion of the launch's hull. He caught a flicker of movement behind one of her small, wood-framed portholes.

For a moment he was tempted to pass by and head in for the jetty. But *Starglow*'s kind usually had owners not likely to settle for second best – and that could mean an angling fanatic who'd use any information he could get about fishing marks, regardless of restrictions. Carrick sighed, swung the packboat's tiller, cut the engine, and drifted down towards the launch.

A minute later he was on her teak decking, faintly puzzled that his arrival seemed unnoticed. He crossed to the cockpit, looked in the open door, and drew a deep breath.

'Hello, down there . . .'

The shout brought a rustle of movement from somewhere below. Then the launch was silent again apart from the gentle gurgle of the water in her bilges.

Carrick's mouth tightened a little as he looked more closely at the open door. The lock seemed intact, but there were faint scratches on the metal just below, and the bolt slot on the doorframe was twisted out of shape. Quietly, he entered the cockpit, glanced round the elaborately fitted interior, and crossed to the narrow companionway leading below.

He listened again, then started down the narrow metal treads.

Halfway, something taut, thin and unyielding bit across his left ankle. Caught off balance, Carrick staggered, fell forward, managed to grab one of the side rails, and ended up on his hands and knees on the deck below. He had a vague impression of a teak-walled cabin, black leather upholstered couches, and a polished silver lamp hanging low from the end of a chain.

The faint sound came from behind him. He started to turn, registered with almost slow-motion surprise that something large and heavy was swinging down towards him then felt an explosion of Technicolor pain inside his skull.

He fell across the bottom of the companionway ladder, while his hat rolled in a short, wild circle.

Chapter Two

A bright blur swung gently and rhythmically. A voice, a girl's voice, was speaking close and urgently.

The haze thinned, the bright blur became the silver lamp on its chain, and Carrick realized he was still lying at the foot of the ladder.

'Oh, hurry up.' The voice sounded again, pleading and impatient. 'Say something if you're all right – anything.'

Carrick eased round with slow care, aware of a drum-like throb within his skull. The girl, in her mid-twenties, was kneeling beside him. Long, flame-red hair caught back loosely at the nape of her neck framed a freckled, oval face, large brown eyes and a wide, presently worried mouth which relaxed in relief as he tried to rise.

'I'll help.' A surprisingly strong arm helped his uncertain progression across *Starglow*'s cabin and he flopped down on one of the deep-upholstered couches. 'You – you're all right?' she queried.

'Give or take a little.' Carrick drew a deep breath and explored his head with tender care. There was a fast-rising lump at the back, but the rest seemed intact. By his wrist-watch he'd been out only a matter of minutes. 'What happened?'

'I – I'll get your hat.' The girl turned quickly away.

He sighed and was content for the moment to watch her go back to the companionway ladder. She was small but well-made, filling to fine proportion an old black vee-necked sweater and a pair of faded blue cotton shorts. Her long, slim legs were bare, her feet were in white plimsolls, and as she bent down the resulting gap between sweater and shorts revealed a honey-tanned inch or so of middle.

'I asked what happened,' Carrick reminded.

'Here's your hat.' She made it sound like an apology as she returned. 'I hit you.'

'You –' He took the hat from her, his mouth still framing the word.

'By mistake. With that –' She waved vaguely towards the short, heavy butt section of a deep-sea big-game rod lying on the opposite couch, then frowned warily. The freckles wrinkled on a pert, turned-up nose. Her ears were small and delicate and there was no trace of make-up on her face. 'I didn't mean to hit you so hard. Or – well, maybe I did. I'm not sure.'

'Let's not argue round it.' Carrick moved his head again and winced. 'Mind telling me why?'

The girl flushed a shade which almost matched her hair. 'Because I thought – well, that you'd come back again.' She stopped, sighed, and tried again. 'Look, I spent the night here on my own. About two a.m. someone had a couple of tries at breaking in. The result is I didn't get to sleep until – oh, I don't know when. Then I wake up with you clattering down the companionway . . .'

'And decide to hit first then find out who I am later?' Carrick raised an expressive eyebrow. 'Do you usually go to bed with your clothes on?'

'When I think I might have a returning visitor, yes.' She nodded towards a huddle of blankets lying just behind the ladder. 'I left the stern cabin and spent the rest of the night there. If he came back I wanted to know about it. Instead, you arrived – but if you'd

28

been newly jerked awake wouldn't you have been liable to decide it was a case of thump or be thumped?' A strand of the red hair had come adrift. She brushed it back defiantly. 'I've said I'm sorry.'

'It was all my fault,' surrendered Carrick wearily. 'But what tripped me?'

'Well . . .' A brief twinkle of something like amusement began in her eyes. 'I'd set up a kind of alarm system, a length of nylon line tied across the siderails on the ladder just above the third bottom tread.'

'It worked,' said Carrick grimly. He fumbled for his cigarettes. 'But I'm not your man.'

'I know.' She settled with a sigh on the couch beside him, legs curled up beneath her. 'I found your warrant card when I went through your pockets. And don't look so surprised, Mr Carrick – I wanted to find out just who I'd clubbed.' She shook her head at the offered cigarette, waited till he'd lit his own, then suggested hopefully, 'Well, if you're not going to have me tossed into jail for assault maybe we could start at the beginning again. I'm Alva Leslie.'

'Hello,' nodded Carrick dryly. If the *Starglow* prowler had returned again and fallen into the waiting trap he could feel almost sorry for him. 'Let's get this straight, Miss –'

'Make it Alva. Everybody does.'

'Everybody you thump on the head?' Carrick's wry-mouthed grin took the sting from the query. 'Is this your boat?'

'No such luck.' Alva Leslie purred at the vision. 'The owner is a Londoner called Abbott, the white-collared business type. He's up with a couple of friends.' One short-trimmed fingernail traced a pattern on the black leather of the couch. 'They asked the festival organizers to name someone with local knowledge who could be hired as extra crew. I heard and volunteered – they get me for free, and in return

I can sleep aboard and fish with them from *Starglow*. That way I'm saving hotel bill and boat charges.'

'Which helps?'

'A lot. I grew up around here, but now I'm strictly a typewriter slave in Glasgow, and this rates as my summer break ... half of it anyway.' She bounced down from the couch. 'Look, I'd get you a drink if I could, but if there's a bottle on board, Abbott has it locked away. I could make some coffee –'

Carrick shook his head. 'Thanks, but not now. About this prowler – what happened?'

Alva Leslie stopped where she was, her mouth tightening. 'The first time I woke up and heard a noise, like a dinghy rubbing alongside. Then somebody seemed to be trying to climb on deck, that stopped, and there was a splash or two as if the dinghy had pushed off again. I thought it was just some wandering drunk trying to get back to his own boat.'

'But the next time?' Carrick drew gently on the cigarette and leaned forward a little.

'That was about half an hour later.' Alva Leslie spoke in the same matter-of-fact fashion, but with an underlying dislike of the memory. 'I was practically asleep again when there were the same noises, then someone began fiddling with the cockpit lock.' She shrugged. 'I waited a moment or two, heard the lock bursting, and decided the best form of defence was a good old-fashioned attack. So I grabbed that rod-end, snapped on the lights, and went charging up.'

'You saw him?'

'Not the way you mean.' The same rebellious wisp of hair had flopped down over her forehead and she brushed it back again with a sigh. 'He must have been almost as scared as I was – when I got on deck all I could see was a dinghy being rowed like mad out into the dark. And I couldn't find the cockpit spotlight's switch. So I just fiddled around with the cockpit lock, decided it was hopeless, and – well, came back down here.'

'And that was the end of it?' He regarded the girl incredulously. 'What about Abbott, or the police –'

'I didn't see much point. My man in the dinghy was well away, the village constable would be snug in bed, and the best idea seemed just to leave things until Mr Abbott showed up this morning. He's staying at the hotel.' She grimaced briefly. 'But I don't mind admitting I stayed awake for long enough. After a spell I even started making up some extra spinners just to keep from dropping off.' She went over to the blanket bed and returned with a small cardboard box. 'There's the results.'

'I'm no fisherman,' he warned, reaching in.

'Careful –'

'Hell!' He brought his hand out quickly and sucked the pinprick of blood welling on his thumb. The box held a collection of wickedly barbed Kirby hooks. Most were in various stages of conversion into cigar-shaped lures, the main ingredients aluminium foil and a short tail of bright red ribbon.

'They're pretty effective,' she said with a touch of pride. 'Put them among bass or pollack and the fish practically queue to be caught.'

'Uh-huh.' He looked again but didn't touch. When it came to artificial lures like the swivel-mounted spinners most anglers had their own ideas. A shortage of soup spoons from *Marlin*'s cutlery chest about a year back had ended when a radioman was found making up spinners from the sawn-off handles. Almost anything from plastic cable covering onwards was liable to be material for the enthusiast. 'Well, let's hope they appreciate this collection.'

'Specially made for the occasion.' She put the box down and asked, 'What time is it now?'

'Around nine.'

'Oh.' Her lips pursed quickly. 'Then Abbott should be along soon. You – it's all right, isn't it? About what happened, I mean?'

'Let's say on condition I can claim a degree of compensation.' Carrick grinned, put on his hat with unusual care, and rose to his feet. '*Marlin's* going to be around Loch Rachan most of the festival. You won't be fishing all the time, will you?'

She shook her head, smiling a little.

'Tonight?'

'There's nothing planned,' she agreed. 'But I'm going to have to find a room somewhere in the village. I've had enough of sleeping out here.'

'The hotel, for a meal, around eight?'

'All right.' Her eyes widened as he started for the companionway ladder, and she made a dive to get there first. 'Wait a minute –'

'Once is enough,' agreed Carrick as she untied the nylon trip-line. 'Well, I'll get on my way.'

She looked suddenly puzzled. 'Why did you come aboard anyway?'

'That?' He shoved his hat further back and grinned. 'It was more or less knocked out of my head. We're going around handing out a gentle reminder to contest boats not to stray too far south. You've had the warning about the Navy's exercise area.'

'Several times. And it's a pity – I could have taken Abbott and his friends to one or two good marks down there.' She stretched in lazy, animal-like fashion and queried, 'What would you do if you did find us there?'

'Chase you off, tow you back if we had to.'

She chuckled. 'Don't worry. Right now I just hope I can stay awake long enough to give them a mild practice session.'

The girl watched him head up towards the deck, then yawned despite herself as she turned to gather the blankets from the deck.

From the jetty's rough boardwalk to the centre of Borland village was only a short stroll. Carrick tied the packboat's painter to a handy mooring ring, clambered up, and walked towards the red brick building which served as post office, general store and local terminus for the twice-daily mail bus from the outside world. Only a few of the angling boats remained, and the village had returned to something approaching its usual sleepy self.

Outside the store, a large mongrel dog lay on its back enjoying the sun. Further along the little street a woman appeared briefly at a cottage door, flapped a tablecloth, and went back inside. A gull swooped low, but planed upwards again as an elderly truck rumbled past.

Carrick stopped for a moment to inspect the store's window, where most of the display space boosted the angling festival. Then he crossed the narrow, cobbled roadway and walked on towards the hotel.

The only building in Borland village to boast three storeys, the Dairg Tower Hotel would have been hard to miss. An old, solid structure of grey granite with traces of green moss on its slate roof, it stood on its own about two hundred yards from the jetty flanked by the church hall on one side and a small, tumbledown garage on the other. The main spread of its windows looked out across Loch Rachan towards the open water beyond. Carrick crunched along its short, gravelled path, pushed through the heavy, oak-framed entrance door, and found himself in a wide, high-ceilinged hallway. The walls were panelled in wood, the carpet leading to the reception desk was an elderly blue, and the main touch of colour was supplied by a fresh series of competition posters.

'Good morning, sir.' The receptionist behind the desk, a dark-haired lass with a lilt to her voice, greeted him with a smile.

'All right, Miss MacDonald, thank you –' a louder voice cut her short and Carrick turned as a strange figure came bustling towards him from the opened door of the residents' lounge. Fat, bald, only about five feet high, wearing a kilt at least two sizes too small with a brown tweed jacket, the little man spoke again in the same high-pitched voice. 'Chief Officer Carrick? Captain Shannon mentioned you'd probably be along. I'm Peter Mack, the owner here – welcome to the Dairg Tower.'

'Thanks.' Carrick kept a straight face as a small plump hand earnestly pumped his own.

'The rest of the competition committee went back with Shannon to visit the fishery cruiser,' declared Mack briskly, his sharp, bright eyes watching the whole sweep of the entrance hall. 'But when you're in the hotel trade you've got to stay with the job, even if you're competition secretary.'

'Some other time, maybe. We can arrange it.' Carrick regarded him warily. Outside of the army, Boy Scouts and comic singers the kilt was a dying rarity in Scottish dress – except when some clan society had its annual shindig. On Peter Mack it was wildly out of character, though complete down to the traditional dress knife tucked carefully into the top of one of the stockings which covered his fat, bulging calves.

The hotelier seemed to read his mind and chuckled. 'Don't worry about the outfit, Mr Carrick. It's on loan for the week – good for business which means good for me.'

'The same applies to the angling festival?' queried Carrick dryly.

'Well, everything helps –' Mack broke off as a cluster of guests came out of the dining room at the far end of the corridor and beamed a greeting as they headed for the stairway and their rooms above. Then he turned back again, his voice dropping a couple of levels. 'This competition could put Borland firmly on the sea-angling maps, Mr Carrick. That's obviously good for the hotel and the whole village.'

'Then let's hope everyone has record catches,' murmured Carrick. 'What's the chances?'

'Good, according to the experts.' The hotelier spread his hands in a blandly admissive gesture. 'But to me, fish are things I serve on plates and anglers are guests like any other – except most of them want breakfast at crack of dawn. I – ah – supported the idea in its formative stages as a business man, that's all.'

The little man's frankness was appealing. Carrick rubbed one hand along his chin to hide a grin, and asked, 'You've a man called Abbott staying here, haven't you?'

'From the big cabin launch out in the loch.' Mack nodded happily. 'With two friends – almost the only party who eat breakfast at a civilized hour.'

'You mean –' Carrick glanced towards the stairway.

'They've just gone up,' confirmed Mack. A note of caution slipped into his voice. 'Is there any – ah – problem involved, Mr Carrick?'

'It can wait.' Carrick thumbed towards the competition posters. 'As secretary, I suppose you've warned entrants about the ban on fishing in the exercise area?'

'Of course.' The hotelier led him over to the reception desk. 'Jean, give me a copy of the regulations.'

The girl laid aside the account file she'd been using, bent below the desk, and bobbed up a moment later with a small, blue-bound booklet. Mack handed it to Carrick.

'It's all in there, Chief Officer. In large type on almost the first page. You can keep that copy if you like.'

'Fine.' Carrick stowed the booklet in his pocket. 'How many entries and boats do you have?'

'Let me see.' The little man fidgeted uncomfortably and eased the tight band of the kilt around his middle to a more comfortable position. 'Two hundred and seven, operating from thirty-two boats. We laid on the two drifters for anglers who couldn't make their own arrangements. Then, of course, there's the *March Wind*, that big sailing ketch. But it hardly counts – it belongs to our committee chairman, Colonel Martin, and he's using it as commodore's yacht.' He glanced past Carrick as a waiter padded towards them. 'Well, Charlie?'

The man shrugged the shoulders of his greasy jacket. 'Nothin', Mr Mack. Want me to keep at it?'

Mack chewed lightly on his lower lip then shook his head. 'I'll see you later.' As the waiter went off, the hotelier sighed.

'Trouble?' queried Carrick.

'No – no, just an annoyance,' declared Mack in a vaguely perturbed voice. He brightened. 'One of our anglers being rather naughty. He didn't turn up at his allocated boat on time – probably teamed up with someone else and didn't bother to let anyone know.'

'Name of Nathan Broom?' Carrick chuckled. 'I was out on the *Blue Vine* when her skipper was creating hell about him being missing.'

'The same.' Mack suddenly lowered his voice. 'If you still want to talk to Mr Abbott, he's coming downstairs now. Wearing the blue jacket.'

Carrick gave a faint nod and glanced towards the stairway. Page Abbott, the owner of *Starglow*, was a slim-shouldered man in his early forties with thinning, mousey hair and a city-pale face. Dressed in an outfit of corduroys, wool shirt and anorak jacket, he was talking quietly to his two companions as they came down together. One was a woman, tall, slender, probably in her late thirties, with prematurely grey hair cut short and tinted blue. Her red denim sailing suit and small matching cap looked both new and expensive. The man just behind them was burly, red-faced with a small moustache, and was dressed in a heavy dark sweater and flannels.

'Mr Abbott –' Peter Mack stepped quickly forward as they reached the hall. 'Going out now?'

'For a spell while the weather holds,' said Abbott easily. 'But I'm betting it breaks down by nightfall.'

Mack blinked in mild protest. 'I hope you're wrong. Ah – this gentleman would like a word with you, if you've a moment.'

'Oh?' Abbott glanced over, saw Carrick's uniform, displayed a mild curiosity. 'What brings the Navy calling at this hour?'

'Fishery Protection,' corrected Carrick, closing the gap between them. 'You've a girl out on your boat, an Alva Leslie –'

'That's right, as extra crew.' Abbott seemed puzzled. 'She was recommended to us by the festival organizers.'

'You knew she was sleeping aboard last night?'

'That's part of the arrangement, isn't it, Page?' declared the woman at Abbott's side.

He nodded. 'Go on, mister.'

'When were you out at *Starglow* last, Mr Abbott?' Carrick noticed Peter Mack sidling close, the little man's face a study in polite curiosity.

'About eleven last night. We left Miss Leslie aboard and came ashore with the dinghy.' Abbott produced a plain silver cigarette case, took out a cigarette, and lit it with a matching lighter. 'We're just going out now.'

'Miss Leslie will tell you she had a visitor about two a.m. He tried to get into the cabin, but she scared him off.'

'You're sure of this?' Abbott left the cigarette in his mouth, his eyes screwed up behind the smoke. 'A girl on her own out there might imagine things.'

The red-faced man behind him grunted agreement.

'It could even have been a fish splashing in the water,' suggested the woman eagerly.

'This particular "fish" jemmied open the cockpit door-lock before he left,' said Carrick softly. 'I've seen it for myself.' He glanced at Peter Mack. 'Have any of the other boats reported a prowler so far?'

'None, absolutely none!' The little man was indignant at the suggestion.

'We'll get straight out there,' growled Abbott. 'But why didn't she get word to us?'

Carrick shrugged. 'She's fairly capable of looking after herself, and thought she'd leave it till you arrived.'

'Which will be right now.' Abbott turned to his companions and jerked his head towards the door. 'Come on – I want to find out more about this.'

They went out, and Peter Mack gave a sighing groan as the main door slammed shut again. 'Carrick, I just hope there won't be a fuss that might harm the festival –'

'Or even worse, be bad for business?' Carrick gave him little sympathy. 'Who were the man and woman with Abbott?'

'Reception can tell you. I – I'm not sure.' Mack looked around with worried eyes. 'Do you mind if I go? I've work waiting.'

'I'll see you again perhaps,' nodded Carrick.

'With happier news next time,' pleaded the hotelier. He gave a slight, anxious bow and hurried off.

His mouth twisted in a grin, Carrick went over to the reception desk. 'Jean, can you tell me who Mr Abbott's friends are?'

The dark-haired girl didn't bother glancing at the register.

'Rooms 304 and 305 – Mrs Margaret Harding and Mr Douglas Swanson. They all booked in two nights back.'

'And Mrs Harding?' Carrick cleared his throat significantly. 'Just how does she fit in?'

'She's a guest of the hotel, Mr Carrick,' reminded the receptionist with a twinkle. 'If she's a widow and if Mr Abbott is paying the bills is it our business?'

'Definitely not,' he agreed solemnly. 'Now, you wouldn't happen to be able to cap all that by knowing where a certain thirsty bo'sun from *Marlin* might be hiding?'

'You mean Mr Bell?' She gave what could have been a giggle. 'Straight down the corridor, turn right, and you'll find the snuggery. He's there, or he was a few minutes ago. There's a notice on the door saying it's closed, but just go straight in.'

'Special dispensation for our Mr Bell?'

'Well, the licensing people say we can't open to the public till eleven, of course,' she admitted. 'But Mr Bell's having a wee drink with Constable Gregor, so I suppose it's legal enough.'

It was the kind of manoeuvre only the bo'sun's heavy Glasgow-Irish hand could have accomplished. Carrick thanked her and headed down the corridor.

The snuggery door was slightly ajar. He pushed it open and found himself in a small, dim-lit room lined with glass cases filled with a variety of stuffed fish, trophies of a generation of anglers. Clapper Bell sat alone at the little dark oak bar, a half-empty pint mug in his hand, another already empty at his elbow.

'C'me on in, sir,' he invited cheerfully.

'Cosy,' admitted Carrick, climbing on to the stool next to him. 'But I heard you had company.'

'The village cop?' Bell nodded wisely. 'Ah, Gregor's a friendly bloke. I went round to his office for a chat, like, an' he brought me here after a bit.' He sipped beer and explained with suitable seriousness, 'We agreed that, och, you need a quiet place if you want to talk.'

'Hmm.' Carrick looked around. 'And what's the magic word for service?'

Bell rapped his mug twice and loudly on the counter. In a moment a shirt-sleeved barman came through a small, curtained doorway behind the bar.

'A dram o' the best for my Chief Officer,' ordered *Marlin*'s bo'sun. 'An' I'll just have another pint to keep him company.' As the drinks were poured he began to pat his pockets hopefully.

'You fumble, I'll pay,' sighed Carrick, accepting the inevitable. He slid the money across the counter, took a first swallow of the whisky, and sat silent, letting the warm glow spread downwards. The barman left.

'Been busy, sir?' Clapper Bell finished the mug he'd been nursing and pushed it aside. 'The local cop was pretty useful – if there's any gossip goin' it comes his way.'

'I know something else that's coming his way,' mused Carrick. 'A character in a rowboat tried a spot of burglary out there last night.'

'That'll brighten up his life!' Bell listened quietly, with only an occasional grunt of interest or amusement, while Carrick brought him up to date. Then he took a long drink from his new pint, smacked his lips, and suggested, 'From the sound o' her, this Leslie girl doesn't need a hook an' line – she could just jump in an' bash the fish wi' that rod-end.'

'Very funny.' Carrick's voice was acid. 'So far the break-in attempt isn't our problem. But it could shape that way if there's any more trouble.'

'Any chance it was Broom?'

'The wandering angler?' Carrick shrugged. 'It could be anyone. What did your policeman pal have to say about the local picture?'

'That this whole festival idea was drummed up by Peter Mack, an' that if it doesn't come off Mr Mack could lose a lot o' money. The other thing is that some o' the lads here are runnin' a book on the winnin' boat. Most are bettin' on one of the locals named Ogilvie, who's usin' a lobster skiff. But there's a fair amount o' money on the two drifters – their skippers know the water around here like the back o' their hands.' Bell paused for another mammoth sip. 'There's only one other entry really quoted. That girl o' yours –'

'Alva Leslie?'

'Uh-huh.' The bo'sun nodded earnestly. 'Seems she was usin' a rod almost before she was weaned. Her father's principal keeper over on Whip Rock an' a mad-keen angler – had the girl memorizin' every fishing mark around the Whip before she was in her teens.'

Carrick winced. Whip Lighthouse was well to the south, in the Sound of Jura, smack in the middle of the exercise area. 'If she coaxes Abbott to take his boat down that way –'

'Then we'll catch her an' Captain Shannon will make them walk the ruddy plank!' Bell drained the last of his beer and gave a polite burp. 'Eh, there's just one other thing. It's about the torpedo.'

'Well?' Carrick slid down from his stool, ready to go.

'The village cop says the locals aren't happy about this exercise area bein' dumped on their laps. The talk is if anyone does find a stray torp, then they'll make damn sure it stays lost.'

'Feeling sour is one thing. But they could be cooking a load of trouble if they tried that kind of game,' said Carrick grimly.

'They'd have to be caught at it,' reminded Bell sagely. He wiped a hand across his mouth and followed towards the door.

The festival committee were leaving for their return trip to the jetty when the packboat came back alongside *Marlin*. Carrick left his companion to secure the little collapsible, headed towards the bridge, and met a thin, glum figure lounging unhappily in the shelter of the radio-room doorway.

'So you're back.' Pettigrew, still sleepy-eyed, scratched the edge of wispy grey hair showing beneath his hat. 'Consider yourself lucky to be clear of that little lot.' The third mate, an untidy, permanently weary figure who'd packed in a desk job and come back to sea at fifty for some reason of his own, thumbed towards the launch now clearing *Marlin*'s side. 'Only six of them, but they made enough noise for sixty. And questions – they left me wonderin' if my ticket's punched or countersunk.'

Carrick's grin was like fuel to Pettigrew's general gloom.

'It got worse, man. Wills forgot to warn anyone there was new, wet paint around the chain locker and we had to practically scrape the stuff off two of them.' Pettigrew shrugged his opinion of the result then yawned. 'Well, it's still not my watch – I'm getting back to my pit while I can.'

'Mr Pettigrew –' The bellow jerked him upright. *Marlin*'s captain stumped nearer, raised a brief eyebrow in Carrick's direction, then gave his attention to the third mate. 'I didn't like the definition on the radar last night. Check it out on all scans, particularly the point six – stationary check here, then when we're moving.'

'But –'

'Yes, mister?'

'Nothing, sir.' Pettigrew went reluctantly on his way. He lived, he'd long ago decided, in a world which gave no thought to the individual.

'Well, now –' Carrick's turn had come. 'I heard there was trouble between you and a drifter.'

'The *Anna B.*' Carrick gave a slight shrug. 'The skipper doesn't love us – *Skua* arrested him a couple of times last year.' He stopped as a familiar sigh and vibration sounded beneath his feet. The compressed air starter, its work done, faded and a gentle purr of diesel exhaust began rising from *Marlin*'s funnel. 'We're going out, sir?'

Shannon nodded. 'Once the launch gets back – I want to make it clear we're not here to swing around a mooring. We'll head south, work down the coast, make one sweep along the fringe of the exercise area, then go into a routine W pattern.' He flicked the edge of the radio-room door with one finger and removed an imaginary speck of dust. 'I'll take her out, then young Wills can take over and I'll hear how you got on.'

A choppy sea and a moderate westerly wind met them in the Sound when, twenty minutes later, they cleared Loch Rachan. Ensign crackling at her stern, an occasional break of spume coming white over her bow, the fishery cruiser settled into a steady, pulsing pace.

On the bridge, Shannon lowered himself from his command chair and went below. Jumbo Wills took over, grinned at the angular rear view of Pettigrew, who was crouching over the radar screen, then glanced at Carrick.

'Enjoy yourself back there?'

'It was interesting,' said Carrick vaguely, his eyes on the cabin launch on the same course about a quarter mile ahead. Abbott's *Starglow* was heading south at an easy rate but, though they were closing, it was impossible to see who was at her wheel. 'One thing, Jumbo – you were wrong about lady anglers.'

'Huh?' Wills raised a doubtful eyebrow. 'I haven't seen any I'd rave about.'

'Keep looking,' advised Carrick. 'But remember they can pack a wallop.'

Despite the puzzled interest in Wills' eyes he didn't elaborate. A few moments later, as he headed for Shannon's day cabin, *Marlin*'s siren gave a brisk, warning blast as she began to draw level with the cabin launch.

By noon they'd clocked up some sixty sea miles and were on the second leg of Shannon's W pattern. Most of the angling boats were apparently contenting themselves with a fairly modest outing, working a handful of fishing marks within a few miles of the mouth of Loch Rachan. One boat, on its own and heading purposefully towards the exercise area, had made a sudden about turn at first sight of the fishery cruiser's silhouette. Later, on the far side of the wide sound, close under the lee of the sprawling island of Jura and near to fifteen miles from the mainland, they came across a bobbing open launch crewed by a seemingly placid elderly couple. But as *Marlin* eased within greeting range the man and woman joined in an outraged, bellowing demand that they 'get that damned ship out of it and stop scaring our fish.'

After that, it was a mild relief when the next leg of the pattern brought them in contact with what Clapper Bell, for one, called 'a spot o' real fishin''.

44

Long and low-decked, out of one of the Ayrshire ports, the seine-netter had a basket hoisted at her foremast to signal her nets were down. The men hard at work on her deck had a market to catch, a week's pay to earn. But a second basket drifted up to her masthead and *Marlin*'s track altered, curving in, skirting the line of yellow floats which traced the nets' underwater pattern.

The two vessels closed, a line was slung, and the offered 'fry of fish', a basket of prime haddock, was hauled aboard the fishery cruiser. They swung apart again as a pound jar of coffee was thrown to the seine-netter's cook. It was part of the unwritten west coast code – just as much as the understanding that the next time *Marlin* might be alongside for a very different reason, with favours on either side forgotten.

An hour later they started another W sweep – back in sight of the mainland, not far from a couple of angling boats patiently working a patch of rock for conger. Jumbo Wills had just joined Carrick for a scratch lunch in the tiny wardroom when the deck suddenly heeled as the ship made a sharp wheel to starboard and the diesels began a rapid increase in tempo. Carrick cursed softly, quickly forked another mouthful of stew, and was still chewing when Clapper Bell stuck his head round the doorway.

'Captain wants you both,' said the bo'sun laconically. 'There's a panic on.'

'What's up?' Carrick rose to his feet, swallowing a mouthful of over-warm coffee. The deck quivered anew as their pace continued to quicken.

'He got a message from the radio room,' Bell told him. 'Somethin' about that torpedo. There's a boat bein' readied an' we're checking the winch.'

By the time they reached the deck *Marlin* was in her full stride, heading south, a foaming wake boiling from her stern. A group of deckhands were already fussing around the smaller of the fishery cruiser's launches, swinging it out on its davits. A slow chatter came from aft as the main winch, the steel cable drum clicking, was given a test run.

On the bridge, Shannon grunted an acknowledgement of their arrival then spun on his heel as Pettigrew emerged from the box-like chartroom.

'Well?'

'Like you said, sir,' nodded Pettigrew, brisk for once. 'Even with low tide, we'll have four fathoms under us until we're close in to the rock. But it's tricky.'

'Right.' Shannon glanced at the attentive helmsman. 'Two points to port, then hold her steady. Mr Wills –'

'Sir?'

'Detail two men to that boat, another two for bridge lookouts. And check the boat's R.T. is working for once.' He rubbed his hands briefly and turned to Carrick. 'There's a shore report – coastguard, I'm told – that something with an orange marker is lying on a reef off the Camas Dubh cliffs. We're heading there now. The Navy think it could be their torpedo, and we're a lot nearer than any of their craft. I've told them we'll take a look and collect or advise.'

'Collect?' Carrick showed his surprise. The standard 21 inch Mk 19 torpedo used by the submarine branch, a hydrogen peroxide drive unit, was approximately twenty feet long and weighed about a ton and a half. *Marlin*'s gear could easily handle that kind of weight on a direct lift, but there was the problem of getting near enough in the first instance.

'Collect it,' repeated Shannon with a positive emphasis. 'Your job, mister. And if –' he corrected himself quickly – 'once we get it, we head straight for the Gareloch Flotilla's base and dump it in the Navy's lap, compliments of Fishery Protection.' The prospect pleased him. 'Better get ready. We'll be off the area inside fifteen minutes.'

His estimate was out by less than a minute. But there was still a need for skilful handling ahead. Standing by the bridge wing, Carrick pursed his lips in a silent whistle as *Marlin*'s speed fell away and she approached the shore at a cautious crawl.

Camas Dubh meant the black channel in the old Gaelic tongue – a channel almost a mile wide, fringed to seaward by an unseen reef and on the shore by the cliffs which gave the place its name.

Two miles of a high, sheer, mostly unclimbable coastal lip of black basalt formed a barrier against which the sea spent its force, except now, at low tide, when a stretch of jagged, weed-greened rock lay half-exposed. Beyond a brief stretch of shallows lay another broken, fissured shelf of the same black rock, the final reef edging the start of deep water. But any chart in existence warned of hidden fingers of rock for some way out before the true passage began, still holding dangers for deep-draught vessels.

Even with the light sea running and despite the hot, mid-afternoon sun shining down, the men on the bridge felt a cold tension. All except Shannon. Sitting in the command chair, his small, stout figure giving an outward impression of relaxed, assured calm, he brought the fishery cruiser in with a series of quiet, unhurried orders. The echo-sounder was working, Pettigrew had the recorder under constant survey, but the protection squadron's senior captain relied on his own feel for water as much as anything. The slightest telltale discolouration, the flecking of an eddy, a variance in the wave pattern around told their own story to his half-shut eyes.

A signal lamp blinked from the cliffs. Carrick swung the bridge glasses and picked out a group of small figures standing motionless. At his side, Clapper Bell spelled out the flickering morse.

'Object . . . your . . .' He waited, while the lamp continued. 'They say we have it at about our ten o'clock, sir.' He gave a sudden grunt. 'Letter U. Repeating.'

'Full astern both,' snapped Shannon almost simultaneously. Letter U had only one meaning in the international code – standing into danger. The cause lay ahead, a deceptively innocent swirl which planed out the shape of each swell that passed.

The telegraph rang, *Marlin*'s wake suddenly frothed and refrothed as she stopped, and the echo-sounder's graph jumped as it traced the start of a fast-rising pinnacle. Slowly, the fishery cruiser backed away. Shannon drew a slow, deep breath. 'Bo'sun, thank our friends.'

They anchored where they were. A minute later, the launch kissed the water, the bow and stern men freeing their davit pins as soon as Carrick, Wills and Clapper Bell had scrambled down to join them.

Another series of signals from the clifftop guided the launch along the edge of the reef until at last they nosed in beside one platform ledge. As the boat's fenders touched, Carrick jumped for the slippery, green-slimed rock followed by Wills and the bo'sun.

From there it was a short, awkward scramble with the occasional minor hazard of a weed-fringed pool.

'Over –' Jumbo Wills gulped and came to a sudden halt, his voice dying away. He pointed, but they'd also seen.

Wedged in a crevice of rock, folded like a jackknife as the tide had deposited him, the dead man was clad in a bright orange sailing jacket. One arm was hidden beneath his body, the other was outstretched like a useless claw. They'd found Shannon's 'torpedo' – and no blame could be attached to the men on the cliff.

From there, all they could have seen would be the sun shining on that bright orange shape, the rest hidden from view.

Together, they splashed ankle-deep across a final sea-pool then stared at the wrinkled, walnut face of the dead man. Clapper Bell swore, hunkered down, and when he glanced round his eyes were bleak.

'Makes it nasty, eh?'

Carrick nodded.

The nylon line used to strangle the stranger had, like most of its kind, first contracted when immersed in the water then stretched beyond its original length once it had begun to dry on the exposed rock. Tiny loops of the line extruded from the deep groove cut into the neck.

And his killer hadn't meant him to be found. A short length of rope tied a pig-iron ballast block round his waist.

Middle-aged, with greying black hair, brown eyes and a faint stubble of beard, the dead man had been of medium height and heavily built.

Mouth set, Carrick knelt down, gently unfastened the orange jacket, and searched the sodden clothing beneath. He found a small wallet in the hip pocket, spread it open, and read the credit card held in an inside plastic cover.

Nathan Broom, the Festival of the Western Seaways' wayward entrant, had been dead long before people started complaining that he hadn't arrived to take his place on the *Blue Vine*.

'Seen this?' asked Jumbo Wills in a strange voice. He was standing about six feet away, the trailing end of the nylon line in his hand. He raised it, bringing the fishing trace, which had been hidden behind a rock, into their sight. On the end of the trace hung a limp, dead two-foot long tope.

'Well, he caught something,' pronounced Clapper Bell with a touch of morbid sympathy. 'But what do we do?'

'Tell *Marlin*, for a start.' Carrick nodded to Wills, and the second mate departed thankfully to use the launch's radio.

Carrick finished his systematic check. There was some thirty pounds in notes in the dead man's wallet, and a gold watch with matching bracelet was fastened to one wrist. The rest was the inevitable clutter found in any man's pockets.

'Fag?' Clapper Bell leaned against the rock, a cigarette in his mouth, another in his outstretched hand. Carrick took it, bent close as Bell scraped a match to life, then drew the smoke deep into his lungs. He rose, crunched slowly across to the dead fish, then suddenly frowned, picked it up, and examined it closely.

The barbed Kirby hook had gone deep into the upper jaw. But the rest of the spinner hung free. It had a homemade body of aluminium foil and a short tail of bright red ribbon.

He laid the fish down and let the cigarette hang loose between his lips. Alva Leslie was the only person he'd ever seen make lures of that pattern. And there was another reason to bring her name into his mind. Two miles away to the south, a guide to the start of the Camas Dubh deep-water channel, a warning of the treachery of the shoals around, the Whip Light stood like a slender finger of white.

'Aye, it's a bad 'un,' muttered Clapper Bell. The bo'sun kicked angrily at the loose shingle. 'An' we've stopped hangin' folk for this kind o' thing. Bloody wonderful, isn't it?'

Chapter Three

The body, they were advised, was to be taken north to Oban, which could provide all facilities. Behind the signal lay a little battle of telephone calls – Campbeltown, to the south, was a shade nearer their position and would have done equally well. But the only quick way to Campbeltown was by air, a certain Crown pathologist in Glasgow didn't like flying, and that expert had dug in his heels for Oban with its direct rail line from the city.

Marlin reached Oban Bay around four p.m., edged in past the wandering small boats filled with holiday-makers from the resort town's multitude of hotels, and finally berthed at the far end of the cargo quay beside a rust-bucket coaster. An immediate procession of callers began crossing her gangway.

The men with the mortuary wagon were first. They arrived and departed quietly, carrying the wicker-work basket shell they used for such jobs. A local reporter, stringer correspondent for half a dozen national dailies, arrived hopefully as they left. Shannon talked vaguely of a floater they'd found on routine patrol, and the man departed, agreeing it might be worth a paragraph, but no more, once the police had established identity.

'If I happened to miss out a detail or two and if he got the wrong impression then it's in a good cause,' mused Shannon a few minutes later as he waved his latest visitors to seats round the wardroom table.

At his side, Webb Carrick viewed the three strangers with a wary interest as the introductions were completed.

Two were Argyll County C.I.D. men. Detective Superintendent Neilson was a sad-eyed, lean-faced man with a starched line in white shirt collars and a neat bow tie. Slightly round-shouldered, with a faint, rather tired smile on his lips, he had said hardly a word since he came aboard. His companion, Detective Sergeant MacNaught, was tall and taciturn with a pair of bushy black eyebrows and a hairy tweed suit, a combination which gave the impression of a rather truculent bear newly wakened from hibernation.

The third man, sitting at the opposite end of the table from Shannon and gazing around through thick-rimmed spectacles with a rather tolerant inter- est, had captain's rings on his uniform sleeves and was Royal Navy to the tips of his immaculately pol- ished shoes. Captain Andrew Penman had been a submarine commander until the day he'd been told it wasn't uncommon for men in their forties to need spectacles. Now he was administration and depot security officer, Gareloch Flotilla – and loathed it.

'First things first, gentlemen.' Shannon opened the slim manilla file in front of him, took out the type- written summary sheets he'd prepared on the way north from Camas Dubh, gave a copy each to Neilson and Captain Penman, then, as an afterthought, pushed one across to MacNaught. 'The facts as we have them to date.'

'Helpful, quite helpful,' murmured Penman, in a note of mild surprise.

'We try to keep control of our situations, captain,' returned Shannon with a touch of malice. 'Fishery

Protection prides itself in not – ah – losing track of things.'

Penman felt the hidden jibe and sniffed a little. 'Yes, I've heard paperwork is particularly important to your people – captain.'

The two policemen seemed unaware of the brief exchange and concentrated on the typewritten sheets. Neilson was the first to look up.

'Concise,' he commented in a surprisingly soft voice. 'But I'd like a little more information on a couple of points.' He swung towards Carrick. 'Chief Officer, you say the fishing lure on the end of the line was similar to the ones this Leslie girl was making. Then you say that you doubt any valid connection.' He stopped, and his sergeant raised one large black eyebrow to complete the question.

Carrick shrugged. 'The knots,' he said shortly. 'The trace was attached to the line by what's called a half blood knot – a fisherman's knot. The line round his neck was part twist, part tangle, and I'm ignoring it. But the rope holding that chunk of ballast round his waist was tied like a shop parcel. It was pretty well ready to slip free.'

'Too sloppy a job for any true angler?' Neilson sighed. 'There are times when fingers can fumble, Chief Officer. We'll talk to the girl and find out more – but there's probably a simple enough explanation.'

'Maybe this prowler who bothered her bumped into Nathan Broom later on and – and –' Sergeant MacNaught stopped, shrugged, and fell silent.

'There's as much sense in that possibility as in any,' murmured Neilson. He leaned forward, his voice crispening. 'Captain Shannon, the other point I need from you – a matter of opinion. You know the tides and currents along that stretch of coast. Where would you say the body was put into the water?'

Shannon scrubbed his short beard with the fingers of one hand, disliking the question and disliking even more the spark of amused anticipation it brought to Captain Penman's eyes.

'I've stuck to facts –' he began doggedly.

'But I need opinions as well,' insisted Neilson. 'I've got to have some kind of a starting point.'

'And so do I,' bristled Shannon. 'Can you tell me how long Broom's body was in the water? Or the buoyancy factor with ballast slung round his middle? Or whether that line snagged anywhere along the way?' He simmered down a little. 'There's a pronounced tidal stream in the Camas Dubh channel. Maximum flow at this time of month is around four knots – but that's a flow north towards high tide, a flow south on the ebb.'

Puzzled, Sergeant MacNaught cleared his throat. 'You mean it could have been wandering about, captain?'

'For want of a better word, yes. From anywhere half a dozen miles north of the channel to half a dozen miles south. Or even in the channel itself.'

Neilson rubbed a forefinger down the tip of his nose. 'But not from Loch Rachan – or where it joins open water?'

Carrick answered for Shannon with an emphatic shake of his head. 'That's another three or so miles north – with a cross-current against it, superintendent.'

Shannon gained fresh support from a surprising quarter. Captain Penman leaned forward with a sigh. 'Superintendent, if the situation was reversed and you knew where a body had gone in and wanted to find it, the task would be theoretically a hundred times easier and still damnably difficult. You might launch a float of the same size and shape, the same calculated buoyancy, and track it in matching conditions – but you wouldn't necessarily succeed.' He grimaced ruefully. 'That's mainly why I'm here. You found something and want to know where it came from – but I've lost something and want to know where it is now.'

'The torpedo, Captain Penman?' Shannon placed a suitable edge of sympathy in his voice. 'Anything special about it?'

'Unfortunately, yes.' Penman removed his spectacles and polished them vigorously on a handkerchief taken from his sleeve. 'It didn't come from a submarine, at least –' he became suddenly cautious – 'well, not in terms of the final delivery system. It came from a Wasp helicopter.'

'Your submarine flotilla lost a torpedo from a –' Superintendent Neilson boggled for a moment, but Carrick and Shannon exchanged a quick glance of understanding. The Navy were proud of their little two-man Westland Wasps, helicopters with a special 'sea-legs' undercarriage which could take a wild pitching deck in its stride up to a forty-two degree angle without sliding. They were for stern flight deck use on frigates, but if the Navy could pack one aboard a submarine . . .

'From a helicopter,' agreed Penman. 'The Wasp packs a double sting, superintendent. Two homing torpedoes, each only about six feet long, weight approximately 550 pounds, yet enough to send a nuclear sub scurrying for cover. The one we lost is an advanced prototype which should have homed on target on a new sonar-pulse principle. Instead –' he shrugged. 'Well, we've lost it. We want it back to find out what went wrong, and we don't want any – let's say outsider to get it.'

'And just what's it got to do with my murder?' asked Neilson, his sad eyes narrowing in almost proprietorial distrust. 'If you're suggesting –'

'Personally, I'm not suggesting anything.' Penman shifted a little uneasily in his chair. 'But the Admiralty feel possibilities can't be ignored. I'm under orders to ensure such possibilities are kept in mind, to ensure there is no security aspect involved and to immediately advise on procedure if there is.'

Neilson pursed his lips. 'I'm always interested in advice on procedure,' he said with an acid sarcasm. 'But until then, Sergeant MacNaught and myself will probably manage.' He folded Shannon's summary, slipped it in an inside pocket, then pushed back his chair and rose. 'Taking *Marlin* back to Loch Rachan tonight, Captain Shannon?'

Shannon nodded.

'Then you'll see us there. We'll drive down.' He glanced at Penman and asked with a chilled courtesy, 'Any particular plans?'

Penman frowned, uncertain. 'I suppose I should see the body –' he began unhappily.

'All right.' The policeman gave a grunt. 'That's next stop on my list. If you come now we can both get it over with.'

They said their goodbyes and left. As the wardroom door closed, Shannon chuckled. He got up, crossed to a locker, opened it, and took out bottle and glasses.

'A drink, Mr Carrick,' he invited. 'Something tells me we're going to need a spot of fortification before this is complete.' He poured a measure of whisky into each glass, added a suspicion of water to his own from the carafe on the table then stopped as he saw the expression on Carrick's face. 'Something troubling you?'

'No, sir.' Carrick chose his words with care. 'I'd just like to know what part we play now.'

'Our own,' said Shannon simply, sniffing his glass with expert approval. 'We co-operate with the shore police, let the Navy weep on our shoulder if they feel so inclined, and make our own inquiries when – well, when we consider it appropriate.' He pushed the second glass towards Carrick, watched with slight distaste as his chief officer added a much more generous quantity of water, then suddenly asked, 'Can you make it your business to see the Leslie girl tonight?'

'We've something arranged,' admitted Carrick.

'Good.' Shannon sipped his glass. 'I'm dining ashore with the festival committee, and I'll find out what they know about Broom.'

'Including Peter Mack?' queried Carrick. 'Right now I'd bet a month's pay against his kilt that he knew Broom hadn't slept in the Dairg Tower last night but decided to keep quiet and hope for the best.'

'I'll see him,' confirmed Shannon. He glanced at his watch. 'You planning to waste much more time down here, mister?'

Carrick quickly finished his drink and followed him towards the bridge.

Loch Rachan mirrored all that was beauty in a West Highland summer evening when *Marlin* arrived back off Borland and anchored once more. It was cool and bright, dusk was still hours away, and only a few dark wisps of cloud on the horizon disturbed the blue of the sky.

At seven-forty, only minutes after her arrival, the fishery cruiser's launch cut a rippling wake across the glass-smooth water towards the jetty. Aboard her with Captain Shannon and Carrick were half a dozen of the crew who'd been given shore leave. They reached the jetty, Shannon strode off briskly towards the hotel, and the liberty men scattered in a prowl to discover just what the village had to offer.

Carrick hung back. Most of the angling fleet had returned to their moorings – *Starglow* was there and he recognized others – while at least two late home-comers were on their way in from the Sound. But tied alongside the jetty, lying only a few yards from where he stood, was a boat of more immediate interest. The *Anna B.*, the drifter which had come so close to running him down that morning, was as drab and dirty viewed from deck level as she'd seemed from the packboat's angle.

He crossed towards her. At the stern, one of the crew was peeling potatoes over a bucket. A cigarette dangling from his mouth, he looked around at the sound of Carrick's footsteps and gave a slow, sardonic glint of recognition.

'Skipper aboard?' demanded Carrick.

'Uh-huh.' The man used the galley knife in his hand as a pointer towards the companionway hatch.

'Right.' Carrick stepped across the gap between jetty and deck. 'Get him.'

For a moment the deckhand didn't stir. Then he shrugged, rose, went over to the open hatch and shouted down.

'Hey, Skinner – you've a visitor.'

A reply rumbled back. The man grinned and saun-tered back to his potato peeling. A moment passed then Skinner Jones came clattering up the iron ladder. The drifter skipper wore an old jersey and overalls, the jersey sleeves pulled up above his elbows. He'd shaved since the morning and seemed to have nicked the skin under one of his high cheekbones in the process.

'You?' He regarded Carrick with a sour surprise then looked around. 'All by yourself? I thought Fishery snoops went in twosomes for safety.'

'Call it a courtesy call,' suggested Carrick dryly. 'Skinner, I don't like comedians.'

'Meanin' this morning?' The *Anna B.*'s skipper chuckled cynically. 'Don't tell me you were worried?'

'Try it again and you'll find out.' Carrick sniffed the stale, rancid odour of long-dead fish which seemed to rise from the drifter's deck and showed his disgust. 'Why don't you give this tub a hosing down now and again?'

'An' why don't you mind your own dam' business?' Skinner Jones stepped towards him, his eyes glinting balefully. One hand grabbed for Carrick's jacket lapel. Carrick knocked it aside, a sudden red rage seemed to explode in the man, and his other hand clawed forward.

Carrick seized the offered wrist in a lock-grip, spun the drifter man round, and shoved him hard against the *Anna B.*'s wheelhouse. Jones recovered, faced him again with his mouth twitching, then dived towards him. As the man came on, one wildly flailing fist connected with Carrick's shoulder – then Carrick, without changing his stance, hit him twice. The first of the two short, deceptively quick blows took Skinner Jones just above the chrome of his overall belt buckle and bent him forward, wheezing. The second took him hard just below the left ear. Jones staggered back, his shoulders met the wheelhouse glass, and he leaned there, mouth half-open and eyes dazed.

'Aye.' The deckhand with the potato knife looked at Carrick then stuck the blade carefully into the wood of the deck. 'Skinner's maybe a wee bit quick-tempered, Chief,' he said anxiously. 'But I'm the peaceful type.'

'Good.' Carrick kept one eye on the skipper, but Skinner Jones appeared to have had enough. 'If you want things to stay peaceful tell him to make sure he doesn't take your cash customers too far south. If he does, we'll chase your tails for the rest of the week.'

'I'll tell 'im,' nodded the deckhand eagerly.

'One other thing.' Carrick's voice kept the same sharp edge. 'Was anyone from here using a dinghy last night – late last night?'

A brief flutter of what might have been fear crossed the deckhand's face. But it lasted no longer than the blink of a camera shutter, then he shook his head. 'Not from here, Chief.'

'All right.' Carrick gave a last glance towards Skinner Jones, who was pulling himself upright and still shaking his head, then crossed back on to the jetty. He set off for the village at a brisk walk, a satisfying ache around the knuckles of his right fist and a shrewd suspicion in his mind that the man had been lying. But the time to concentrate on the latter point would come later.

The Dairg Tower was busy with guests when he arrived, most of them either on their way to dinner or gossiping in the foyer as a prelude to moving on to the cocktail bar. Carrick eased through the bustle towards the reception desk, where the dark-haired Jean MacDonald was on duty.

'Jean, I'm looking for –'

'Alva?' She nodded cheerfully. 'She told me. You'll find her in the snuggery bar – it's a shade quieter.'

He thanked the girl, headed along the corridor and pushed open the door at its end. The snuggery was a smoke-filled scene, with about a score of people talking and drinking within its restricted space. Alva Leslie was perched on a stool at the far end of the bar counter, a rather subdued expression on her face as she listened to the talk around her. Carrick began to ease his way across the room, then stopped as a hand fell on his arm.

'Back again?' Page Abbott wore a dark lounge suit and had a glass in his hand. The owner of the *Starglow* seemed in a cheerful mood as did the red-faced Swanson by his side. 'What is it this time, Carrick – business or pleasure?'

'Maybe a little of both,' said Carrick vaguely. 'How was the fishing?'

'Wonderful.' Abbott ran a hand over his mousey hair and his pale face twitched at the memory. 'That girl knows her stuff. Took us south of the loch for a couple of miles then told me to cut the engine and start fishing. I get my rod in the water and – wham, I'm into a ten pound coalfish.'

'A nice start.'

'And just a start!' Abbott shook his head in open admiration. 'Between there and a couple of other places she showed us we were just hauling 'em out all the time. Then she says she knows better places, but that they'll keep till the competition starts tomorrow!'

'Let's hope she does,' grunted Swanson, his forehead glistening with perspiration in the heat of the room. He stopped and nudged Abbott. 'Here's Marge.'

Mrs Harding, poised and cool in a dark red cocktail dress with a single strand of pearls at her throat, moved towards them from the door. She smiled silently at Abbott then looked expectantly towards Carrick.

'Sorry,' said Abbott quickly. 'Carrick, we didn't have time for introductions this morning –'

They went through the formalities. Margaret Harding contented herself with a faintly aloof nod. A good-looking woman, attractive and knowing it, decided Carrick. And from Abbott's manner, she had no need of any admiration society. Swanson's handclasp was as he'd expected, hot and beefy.

'Like a drink, Marge?' queried Swanson.

She shook her head. 'I'd rather eat – blame the sea air.'

'Fine,' agreed Abbott, then glanced at Carrick. 'Well, maybe we'd better get through. That dining room's pretty busy.'

Carrick nodded. 'All set for tomorrow?'

'Organized at any rate,' said Abbott. 'So once we've had a meal we're going to do some sightseeing – we've hired what passes for a car from the local garage.'

'Four wheels and an assortment of rattles,' said Swanson cynically. 'Let's go, Page.'

Carrick watched them head towards the door, then made his way along the bar.

'I'm late,' he said apologetically.

'I heard why.' Alva Leslie grimaced a little. She wore a throat-high sleeveless dress in a bottle-green wool, her copper red hair brushed long then held by a clasp of white ivory at one side. 'It must have been nasty. I've never seen a dead man, but –'

Carrick nodded. 'Who told you?'

'Constable Gregor.' She frowned. 'I've to "hold myself available" to talk to a couple of detectives – about last night, and whether there could be a link.'

'I've met them. They're all right.' He beckoned the barman, and, once Alva had settled for a vodka in lime, ordered a whisky for himself. A moment later a corner table became vacant and they moved across.

When they were seated, he offered her a cigarette, took one himself, lit them both, then regarded her thoughtfully.

'Do I pass inspection?' she asked with a mild touch of humour.

'Uh-huh.' He leaned forward a little. 'Alva, did you know this man Broom?'

'Constable Gregor asked me that too.' Her eyes frosted a little. 'The answer's no – and maybe I had the wrong idea about why you came.'

Carrick shook his head wearily. 'Alva, did you hear how Broom died?'

She blinked. 'Well, he was found washed up on the rocks at Camas Dubh –'

'And he'd been strangled.' He heard her draw a quick intake of breath, saw the fingers tighten round her glass, and went on with a grim, quiet emphasis. 'The killer used a length of nylon line, Alva. It had a homemade lure still attached at one end, a lure with a scrap of red ribbon as a tail.'

'One of mine?' She moistened her lips, a blend of horror and disbelief in her eyes. 'And – and that's why they're coming to see me?'

He nodded. 'We're working with them. Alva, how could someone have got that lure?'

'I don't know. I brought one or two with me, then made up the rest, but –' She stopped and frowned. 'I remember now. I did give one away, to a man on the jetty.'

'What man?'

'Just – just a man, an angler. Middle-aged, dark hair, fairly heavily built –'

'Sun-tanned?'

'Yes. And his face was wrinkled a lot. Then – yes, he looked as though he hadn't shaved for a few days.'

Carrick sighed. 'That was Nathan Broom. Tell me about it.'

'All right.' She took a quick, nervous puff at her cigarette. 'It was yesterday afternoon. I was on the jetty, waiting for Mr Abbott and the others to come down from the hotel, and he came along. We started talking, and he told me he'd already been rock-fishing for a few days.'

'Near here?'

63

'Up and down this part of the coast,' she agreed. 'He mentioned one spot and asked me if I knew it. I did – I sometimes went swimming near there when I was school age. Then he started to ask about the boats in the festival –'

'Any boat in particular?'

'One, yes. He seemed interested in the *Anna B.*'

'You're sure?' Carrick was surprised. 'He was scheduled for the other drifter.'

She shrugged. 'He wanted to know who owned the *Anna B*. Then he talked about fishing, and asked what bait I'd be using. I showed him one of the lures, he liked it and – well, I gave him it. He went away soon after.'

'Think carefully,' he urged. 'Did he say anything that seemed odd?'

A tweed-clad visitor brushed past, almost colliding with their table, and Alva's hand flew instinctively to protect her glass. 'Just one thing,' she said slowly. 'It was when I gave him the lure. He laughed and said he hoped it would bring him luck.' Her brow furrowed. 'Then he said he'd already come close to landing a big fish of his own, and something about it being a very different kind of contest.'

'Nothing else?' Carrick saw her shake her head and didn't press the matter. If Nathan Broom had come north with more than the angling competition in view it was going to take more than a casual probing to discover his reasons. 'One other thing, Alva. Were any of the boats on the move late last night?'

'After dark?' She stubbed her cigarette. 'Yes, quite a few were night fishing.'

'Including the drifters?'

'No – at least, I don't think so.' Alva bit her lip gently. 'Webb, why was Broom killed?'

Carrick shrugged. 'I don't know. There's a suggestion he may have bumped into your prowler, but nothing firm.' Another thought struck him. 'Are you still living out on *Starglow*?'

'Not after last night's business,' she said firmly. 'I managed to get a room in the village – with an old dragon who started off by warning she doesn't allow male visitors.'

They finished their drinks, moved through to the dining room, managed to locate a table in a corner by one of the windows, and settled to their meal. The Dairg Tower menu was reasonably good but the service slow – the committee dinner upstairs, explained their waiter apologetically, was making things difficult.

The extra time gave Carrick a chance to learn more about the red-haired girl opposite him. She'd been born in one of the unique lighthouse villages on the north-west coast, places where every husband or father was in the lighthouse service and any man at home was on leave from some lonely rock station. She'd come to live near Borland in her early teens.

'That was when dad was first moved to the Whip Light,' she mused. 'We had a cottage near the shore, and on a clear day I'd kid myself I could see the lighthouse.'

But her mother had died, she'd been sent to live with an aunt down in Glasgow, and she'd stayed there in the city except for the occasional holiday trip north.

'Planning to see your father?' asked Carrick.

'Uh-huh.' Her eyes sparkled. 'I always do – in fact, we were going to have a try at this festival business together, but then the competition dates were changed for some reason and he couldn't get his leave altered to fit.'

About her companions on *Starglow* she knew little. Abbott had told her vaguely he was in 'stocks and shares' and that the red-faced Swanson was a business friend. Alva wrinkled her nose at the mention of Margaret Harding.

'The lady Marge has already hooked the only fish she wants around here,' she said sardonically. 'But I wonder – the same Mr Abbott has shown a touch of temper a couple of times when she wasn't around. Swanson, now –' she sighed despairingly – 'he's got a brand new set of angling gear and doesn't know one end of a rod from the other.'

Carrick started to chuckle, looked past her, and changed his mind. He glanced at his watch. 'Any plans for the rest of the evening?'

'I'm supposed to "hold myself available",' she reminded. 'I don't know when these detectives will arrive.'

'They're here.' He thumbed towards the door, where Superintendent Neilson and his sergeant had made an appearance and were frowning in their direction. 'See them, then maybe I can come up with some idea – if you're interested.'

'If I'm not locked up,' she corrected. 'All right. But what kind of an idea?'

'You mentioned a place where you sometimes went swimming –'

'Yes.' She wasn't taken in. 'The same place Broom talked about. Which is it, Webb, business or pleasure?'

'Well, I'd hate to say I'd be killing two birds with one stone.' He grinned disarmingly. 'But how do we get there?'

'I'll fix it,' she sighed. 'Give me half an hour once the inquisition finishes.'

He nodded, they rose, and headed together towards the door.

Superintendent Neilson had taken over the Dairg Tower's cash office as his temporary interview room, and went to pains to guide Alva Leslie to the more comfortable of the two chairs available. Behind them, Sergeant MacNaught slouched over to the window, notebook and ballpoint unobtrusively ready.

Neilson turned briefly towards Carrick. 'You've talked to her about it?' he asked, as if already certain of the answer. Carrick nodded, and the policeman sighed. 'And Shannon has had a session with Peter Mack – well, it's our fault, I suppose. We should have been here sooner.'

'You've seen Mack?' queried Carrick.

'First on our list,' confirmed Neilson. There was more than a touch of peeved resentment in his voice, and behind him Sergeant MacNaught's lips twitched in a guarded grin. 'Captain Shannon had him in a comer when we arrived, then told us we could take over – that it was time he went on to the committee dinner!' With an effort, he kept his feelings under control. 'Let's talk about that later. For now, I want to hear Miss Leslie.'

Neilson began. Slowly, methodically, he led Alva through her story once again. A silent spectator, Carrick smoked a cigarette and listened. No one could have described Neilson as a sparkling thruster, but he certainly knew his job when it came to acting as interrogator – and an interrogator, guessed Carrick, who could turn on the pressure when necessary.

At last he was finished and Sergeant MacNaught flipped his notebook shut.

'We'll want you to sign the usual formal statement later, Miss Leslie,' said Neilson in a more friendly voice. 'If you remember anything more then, of course we'd like to know.' He flickered a glance towards Carrick. 'And we'd like to know at least as soon as other people.'

'You mean I'm finished?' She rose to her feet with a sigh of relief. 'It wasn't as bad as I expected.'

'Like visiting the dentist,' agreed Neilson gravely. 'The worst is before it happens.' He raised a thin finger as Carrick made to follow Alva towards the door. 'You'll be back, Chief Officer?'

Carrick nodded. Then, outside in the main hallway, the door closed behind them, he chuckled.

'What's so funny?' demanded Alva, bewildered.

'Just that sooner or later the Old Man and Neilson are going to have a head-on collision – and I'd like to be there when it happens.' Carrick grinned again at the idea, and followed her down the hallway. 'Once you're ready, where do we meet?'

'Near the jetty, round about the general store,' she suggested.

'Fine.' He went with her to the main door, watched her walk down towards the road, then took a deep breath and returned to the office.

Neilson and his sergeant had company. Peter Mack was sitting on a chair by the window, his round face flushed. The kilted hotelier, dwarfed by the two C.I.D. men, was bristling with indignation yet showed a touch of underlying fear.

'You're back at a good time, Carrick,' said Neilson dryly. 'Mr Mack feels we're being unkind.'

'Try and understand how I feel,' began the hotelier unhappily, fingers playing against the hilt of his little ornamented stocking knife. 'You must –'

'Must?' Neilson cut him short and took a step nearer. 'Mack, you're in trouble up to your fat neck. When Carrick was here this morning you already knew Broom hadn't been in the hotel overnight – and as competition secretary you knew he was missing from the practice session.' He rapped one fist on the desk in front of him and turned to Carrick. 'And you told him there'd been a prowler trying to break into one of the boats, correct?'

68

'I told him,' confirmed Carrick unemotionally. 'And he hoped there wouldn't be a fuss.'

'Because of the festival, and the hotel –'

Neilson scowled. 'You were in a position to put one and one together, Mr Mack – but instead you kept quiet. Do nothing, hope for the best, that's what you decided.' Ignoring the man, he explained for Carrick's benefit, 'Broom's bed wasn't slept in. His suitcase had gone – but this character kept it all to himself until the local constable came round this afternoon and told him you'd found the body.'

'I don't run to the police every time a guest goes off without paying his bill,' protested Mack weakly. 'If I'd known he'd been murdered –' He licked suddenly dry lips at the thought of what it might all mean. 'In a place like Borland everyone will have the story by morning. Maybe – yes, maybe we should cancel the festival. It might look better, proper respect for the dead.'

'No.' Neilson was emphatic. 'I want this bunch kept together in one place as long as possible. The odd few may decide to pack up and go if there's a murderer on the loose, but the majority will stay. Cancel the competition and they'll scatter home to all over the country.'

'Aye,' agreed Sergeant MacNaught. 'Keep everything goin' as if nothing had happened.' He glared at the hotelier. 'That should be easy enough for you.'

Mack swallowed. 'All right, I'll try.' He looked hopefully at Neilson. 'Is – is that all?'

'For now,' said Neilson shortly. 'We'll be staying in Borland. That means we'll need a couple of rooms here.'

'I haven't –' Mack corrected himself hastily. 'We'll manage something, I'm sure.'

Neilson nodded, waited until Mack had gone, then

sighed as Sergeant MacNaught closed the door. 'His kind don't help.'

'And my kind?' queried Carrick.

'Yes, I was coming to that.' Neilson leaned back against the desk, frowning. 'I'm a landsman cop who just happens to have been stuck with this case. I've got the Navy round my neck because of it, looking for their damned torpedo. I've got – well, let's be polite and say the unsolicited help of the Fisheries Department, though I'd have thought they'd enough of their own troubles.' He smiled a little bleakly. 'How would you feel?'

'That maybe we either all work together or hang separately,' murmured Carrick, tongue in cheek. 'It could be good insurance, particularly when we don't know what we're handling.'

Neilson shrugged. 'Maybe. This mystery prowler business is just too smooth an explanation for my liking, and this luggage vanishing from Broom's room worries me.'

'No reports of thefts in the village or among the other boats?'

Sergeant MacNaught stirred and answered. 'Nothing ashore. But since the story about the *Starglow* got around the local cop has had one or two boat people coming forward. They're people who've been living on their boats, and they've heard somebody prowling around the moorings in a dinghy late at night.' He sucked his teeth in disgust. 'Nobody told anyone till now – as usual.'

It was the old, old story. The more law-abiding a citizen, the less he liked the idea of getting involved in anything. Carrick rubbed a hand along his chin.

'You've checked on Broom?'

'Preliminary stuff,' nodded Neilson. 'Unmarried, worked in an electronics plant near Edinburgh – nothing to do with torpedoes, thank heaven – and a

mad-keen angler. Good characte
and he was on a two week holida
a couple of nights back, the roo
advance at the same time as he post
entry.'

'None of which helps you much,'
'What about the rest?'

'He had a car, a red Morris Mini. It v
the hotel car park last night.' For a
policeman stood silent, his lips pursed.
that's it. The car's description is circulat
have the full post mortem report on Broom
morning.'

'There's a fingerprint team on its way,' vo
Sergeant MacNaught. 'They'll check the hot
and that boat *Starglow* –'

'I went through Broom's pockets,' said (
softly. 'If there had been any sort of a lead –'

'Then whoever killed him would have taken ca
remove it,' growled Neilson. 'Well, we've more in
views to wrap up. What are your plans?'

'Fairly vague,' confessed Carrick. 'But – yes, y
could say I'll be keeping an eye on a witness.' H
waved one hand in a vague salute and beat a fast
retreat.

The sun was low on the horizon and Loch Rachan was
taking on the first pale pink tinge of early dusk. The
tide was on the turn, and slow, lazy waves were creeping up the shingle with a gentle, hypnotic rhythm and
an easy rustle of shifting pebbles.

Carrick had strolled once and back along the length
of the village. Now, near the jetty, he leaned against a
metal rail which separated the road from the beach
below and lit a cigarette. A flight of skuas were vigorously dive-attacking a patch of water, the signal that

hool of mackerel were out there, travelling close to
surface. A transistor was blaring out music aboard
e of the competition boats, and, further away,
arlin's grey shape had swung round with the tide
ntil it was almost bow-on.

Somehow, it was all a strange, distant world from
hose few hours back when he'd helped bring that
stretcher and its grim burden from the rocks of Camas
Dubh to the waiting launch.

'Grand evening,' declared a gruff voice.

He looked round, and the tall, lean figure of Jenkins
Batford crossed to join him at the rail. The *Blue Vine*'s
skipper stared seaward, a pensive look on his leathery
face.

'Weather looks as though it will hold,' said Carrick
eventually. 'All ready for the morning?'

Batford nodded, and the tassel of his woollen
stocking-cap flapped vigorously. 'What needs done is
done.' He sniffed, and drew the cuff of his shirt along
his nose. 'The word's around you had a busy day
yourself – and I'm not meaning that wee interlude wi'
Skinner Jones.'

'How is he?' asked Carrick.

'Bruised.' Batford's grey eyes twinkled briefly, then
sobered. 'So I'll have one less passenger tomorrow,
eh?'

'Worried about it?'

'Not that way,' said the fisherman tersely. 'No, I just
thought I maybe should have a wee word with you.'

'About Broom?'

'And the rest. You're –' Batford frowned awk-
wardly – 'well, nearer to our kind than those police.'

Carrick said nothing. A fisherman usually set his
own pace, and once his mind was made up nothing
could hurry him.

'Let's say I wouldn't be too sure that what you're
after is here,' mused Batford. 'We've been around

these parts for the past week or so, an' only involved with these angling folk since yesterday. We were doing the usual – a few tries wi' the nets, a few boxes o' whitefish for the Ayr market, an' the prices close to blasphemy.' He paused. 'If a man chooses to run a powerboat out in the Sound late at night without lights – and night after night – I wouldn't normally say anything.'

'Except when there's murder,' agreed Carrick. 'How often?'

'Two nights for certain, maybe three, an' always south of here. I've heard him, but I've never seen him.' Batford moved away from the rail. 'Well, I'll be on my way.'

Carrick flicked the stub of his cigarette towards the shingle below. 'Jenkins –' he spoke casually, almost to himself. 'You know the Navy has lost a torpedo out there, a fairly special one?'

'There's that story around too,' agreed the fisherman reticently.

'That's all you've heard?'

'Should there be more?' The grey eyes regarded him calmly for a moment, then Batford gave a slow, polite nod. 'Good night to you, Mr Carrick.'

He walked away. Carrick was still watching him go when the whine of an approaching engine came from the opposite direction. As he turned, Alva Leslie brought the dusty green motor scooter she was riding to a halt at his side. She wore her 'working outfit' of sweater and shorts, her red hair was crammed under a white crash hat, and she laughed at the expression on his face.

'Transport,' she said proudly over the erratic putter of the exhaust. 'And all my own – ready to go?'

'On this?' The two-wheeler had seen better days, and its Plexiglas windshield had a long crack running down one side. The newest thing about it were the twin canvas pannier bags slung one on either side of the rear wheel.

'Why not?' she asked in mock indignation. 'It brought me up from Glasgow in one piece. Of course, if you're scared –'

He grinned and swung on to the pillion behind her.

'Hold on,' invited the girl. 'No – not like that.' She gave him a quizzical look and moved his hands higher up her waist. Then she twisted the throttle grip, the two-stroke's exhaust came thick and oily, and they were off.

Chapter Four

The tarmac road skirted the head of Loch Rachan like a narrow, dusty ribbon then cut inland and climbed through empty, heather-clad moorland until finally the little Lambretta topped a long rise. The whole width of the Sound of Jura lay ahead, sparkling like fire in the gathering sunset with the distant islands silhouetted like black coals in its midst.

The scooter whined on, the road now hugging close to the coast with an occasional cottage as the main man-made landmark. The only other vehicle they met was an old farm truck laden with sheep, and soon afterwards Alva eased back on the throttle. The Lambretta swung off the tarmac and bounced its way along a rough track towards the shore. She stopped the machine where the track petered out near a thick patch of gorse and grinned as Carrick dismounted.

'Well, was it so bad?'

'I almost enjoyed it,' he said warily, stretching his cramped muscles and looking around. 'Is this the place?'

'Yes.' She propped the scooter on its stand and slung her crash hat by its strap from one handlebar. 'It doesn't have any official name, but I used to call it Silver Cove.'

It was apt. Two arms of land formed a rough crescent, with long fingers of rock at their tips running into the sea.

Sheltered between the arms, shelving quickly into deep water, the cove was edged with what any child with imagination would have called silver sand, fine, white and pure – only a scientist could have been cold-blooded enough to pin it down as silicified wood, the kind of odd outcrop found in a few scattered spots along the West Highland coastline.

'Like it?' she asked.

'Perfect,' he agreed. 'Where was your home, Alva?'

'About a mile north. Then the Camas Dubh channel starts about four miles south of here. Webb –'

Carrick nodded. He'd already seen the sets of tyre tracks on the soft ground beside the gorse. The same car had been driven down the track and had turned at the spot on several occasions. 'Looks like he was here all right. Where would he fish?'

She pointed. 'Probably off the north rocks – I'd say it was the best spot.'

He swung the scooter's pannier bags over one shoulder and together they made their way down towards the beach, scrambling over the rocks.

'There's a cave, just a little one but dry,' declared Alva as they dropped down on to the soft, fine sand. 'He might have used it.'

She led the way with a familiar assurance to where a large boulder lay close to the main rock fringe. Behind its shelter, the cave was a shoulder-high crack in the rock, a crack twice the width of a man and running back some twenty feet. A small ring of stones had been built just outside the entrance and the black ash of a driftwood fire lay within their circle.

Carrick knelt, rubbed the cold, powdered ash between his fingers, and was satisfied. The fire had been recent, within the past few days of dry weather. Any touch of rain would have porridged the ash and told its own story.

76

'There's a torch in one of the panniers,' said Alva quietly, a strange expression on her face.

He found it, switched on the beam, and explored the dark recess of the cave. An empty coffee can lay in one corner, there were a few cigarette stubs on the sandy floor, and he saw a hollow scraped to one side, the type of hollow an experienced camper might fashion for his hip before settling down in a sleeping bag.

They went back out into the open and Alva shivered a little.

'It felt – well, strange in there,' she said apologetically. 'Not because somebody else had used it but because of what happened to him.'

Carrick nodded his understanding but said nothing. They spent the next half-hour in a methodical search of the cove from one arm of rock to the other without any real success. At last he stopped and looked back at the trail of footprints they'd left across the sand. The sun had gone down, the sky was clouding, and dusk was edging in.

'Still like that swim?' queried Alva suddenly. Without waiting for an answer she took the panniers, rummaged in one, and handed him trunks and a towel. 'Yours – courtesy of Jean back at the Dairg Tower. They belong to her brother.'

As Carrick examined them she began peeling off her jersey and shorts, revealing the plain, one-piece costume she wore beneath. A moment later she kicked off her shoes and was ready. 'Hurry up,' she ordered.

He nodded and grinned as she ran down the sand and into the water. Then he stripped down quickly, pulled on the trunks – they were a reasonable fit – and followed, wading out into the rippling waves until he was thigh deep then swimming. He stopped, floated for a moment, saw Alva moving in a smooth overarm crawl further out, and set off after her. She waited until he was close, laughed, then sunfished down in a sudden dive.

Carrick followed her down, staying close to her slim, fast moving figure then suddenly almost lost her among the swaying, living strands of bottom weed. She came back towards him, flipped over in a neat backward roll, and began rising.

Their heads broke surface in the cove almost side by side. She gasped for breath, and, eyes sparkling, pushed the wet hair back from her forehead.

'Something to show you – I've just remembered.' She dived again, Carrick following once more, and this time she swam fast and arrow-straight, the bottom of the cove as familiar to her as a well-memorized map. A dark bulk loomed ahead in the dull green light and she signalled towards it with one hand. Carrick sank down beside it on the pebbled bottom and touched the long, corroded shape with one hand. There were many ways in which an ancient brass cannon could have come to that stretch of coast, but to be led straight to one was a surprise. It might be anything from a relic of the Armada to a reminder of the old privateer days.

She tapped his shoulder, pointed to herself, and then upwards.

'When did you find it?' he asked a moment later, as they floated side by side on the surface.

'Years back, but I never told anyone,' she confessed. 'I always hoped there might be a treasure chest lying around, but there isn't – I checked every inch and there's only some old pottery and other stuff.'

They swam lazily for a spell longer then, as the dusk thickened into darkness, headed almost reluctantly for the beach. They were walking ashore, still almost waist-high, when Carrick stopped and pulled her gently towards him. She came willingly, her lips soft and exploring, her body close against his own, then suddenly drew back a little and rubbed one finger across his chin.

'Enough is enough, Webb. Anyway –' she wrinkled her nose with a touch of humour – 'stay like this and I could end up with pneumonia.'

They continued to the beach, gathered up their clothes and, screened by a handy ledge of rock, towelled down and dressed in silence. When Alva stepped out again, her hair rubbed dry and combed out like a coppery mane, Carrick had a cigarette lit and ready for her. They sat together on the sand, Carrick feeling the warmth of her body against his own, the night now velvet dark and the moon showing only fitfully between the clouds.

'I'll have to go soon,' sighed Alva lazily. She gave a long, cat-like stretch which seemed to ripple from the tips of her toes all the way to her fingernails. 'Even as it is, that landlady will have her suspicions.'

'Uh-huh.' Carrick was already sitting upright, his face holding a frown of puzzled concentration.

'What's wrong?'

He shook his head in silence, listening. Somewhere out in the Sound, heading towards them, a boat engine was throbbing. It couldn't be far distant, half a mile away at most, yet there was no sign of its navigation lights. He glanced at Alva, she nodded her understanding, and they waited.

Another minute passed, the boat's engine coming nearer, the characteristic beat of a kerosene unit growing louder. Then a sudden blink of light, twice repeated, more the loom of a beam than the direct light itself, came from the shore to the north. Almost immediately a signal lamp gave three answering flashes from out in the Sound and the engine slowed.

Carrick swore softly and scrambled to his feet. 'What's to the north of here, Alva?'

'A stretch of foreshore, then another cove.' She'd already followed his example.

'Deep water?'

'Right into the rocks, except for a couple of patches of shingle.'

They set off at a rapid pace, at first keeping to the sand then scrambling over the rocks to the heathery moorland above. The boat in the Sound seemed to have stopped coming in, its engine only ticking over. Carrick stumbled over a hummock in the ground, almost fell, and was starting off again when Alva grabbed his arm.

'Webb –'

The light along the shore was shining again. But now it had resolved itself into the twin glare of headlamps from a car parked somewhere close to the water's edge. Seconds later the harsh note of an outboard engine rasped to life and was immediately throttled back. They hurried on, the moon filtering through the clouds to guide them across the moorland.

Then, close to the edge of the shore, Carrick came to a halt. From where they stood they could look across the full curve of a smaller cove. The fringe glow of the car's headlamps was just enough to reveal the outline of a small power boat moored beside a shelf of rock.

One vague figure was already aboard and another was heading along the rock shelf towards it. The car was about thirty yards away, on higher ground, but its occupants were invisible behind the headlamps' glare.

'I'll get closer,' said Carrick softly. 'You wait here.'

She shook her head stubbornly. 'I know the place, remember?'

He gave in with a faint grin and started forward again, Alva a pace behind, his every sense alert. But what happened next still took him off guard. Less than a handful of yards on, the ground seemed to explode beneath his feet in a frantic squawk, followed by a beating of startled wings. Then the giant gull was flapping skywards, screaming its anger at such a shock awakening.

The car's headlamps went out. A moment later a spotlight flicked on, the narrow beam lancing in their direction. It swung briefly, found them, and the car's horn blared. Sheer instinct took control as Carrick grabbed the girl, dragging her by the wrist towards the shelter of a patch of boulders. As they reached the rocks, the flat, angry blast of a shotgun sounded from the direction of the powerboat. As they dropped down into cover the other barrel followed and the rock above their heads was sprayed with pellets.

They hugged the ground while the outboard's engine rose to a new pitch then changed as it got under way. Simultaneously, the beam of the spotlight went out, the car's engine growled to life, and they heard wheels crunch on shingle.

Carrick rose to his feet in time to see the car drive off, travelling fast, a lightweight boat-trailer bouncing along at its tail.

'All gone?' asked Alva, rising shakily to her feet.

'In a hurry – thanks to that damned bird.' He could still see the phosphorescent wake of the powerboat, heading fast out to sea and the other vessel.

'I can't say I'm sorry.' She dusted herself down in rueful fashion. 'I like people to be friendlier. Well, what now?'

'We'll take a look around.' Carrick pulled the torch from his pocket and led the way. Where the car had stood there were faint tyre marks and a few drops of sump oil. Other tyre marks, wider spaced and belonging to the boat-trailer, led to the wide ledge of rock, where the water lapped quietly. He found an empty four-gallon jerrican lying on its side. Another sign of the rush to leave was the powerboat's mooring rope, slashed loose with a knife and leaving most of its length still secured to a knob of rock.

'Careful,' murmured Alva as he went nearer the edge where a green slime of weed began. 'It's deep down there, even when the tide's out.'

He nodded, and walked further along the shelf, playing the torch beam from side to side. The green slime thickened as the shelf dipped below high water mark, and the rock itself was less regular in surface. The torch beam shone on a spot where the slime had been scraped in some contact which had left the bare surface exposed beneath, then Carrick frowned as the light sparkled back at him in a glitter of red. He went over, stooped, and when he rose up a moment later he held half a dozen tiny fragments of red diamond-like glass in the palm of one hand.

'Alva –'

She looked at them and suggested, 'Someone bashed in a tail light. The boat-trailer maybe?'

'Maybe.' Carrick went to the edge, lay flat on the rock, and shone the torch down into the water. It was difficult to be certain, but there seemed to be something down there on the bottom, something which meant an even better explanation for the fragments.

'Alva, can you find your way back to the scooter?'

'Yes.' She showed surprise that there could be any question involved. 'Why?'

'I'm staying,' he said slowly. 'I'd bet six months' pay they won't be back, but it's maybe better to keep an eye on things. I want you to get back to Loch Rachan, find Captain Shannon, and tell him what happened. Say I think we've found Broom's car but that I'll need the scuba gear.'

She nodded, started to leave, but came back, stood on tiptoe, and kissed him lightly. Then, without a word, she went off into the darkness.

Carrick had to wait from close on midnight until scant minutes off one-thirty a.m. before *Marlin*'s launch arrived and, searchlight blazing, crept cautiously into the cove. He signalled her over to the ledge then, as her rope fenders bumped against the rock and two of her crew secured lines, he stepped aboard. Jumbo Wills waved a greeting from the cockpit.

'What kept you?' asked Carrick sardonically. 'I could have made better time with a sand barge.'

'Not my fault,' declared Wills, grinning in the shaded glow of the cockpit lights. 'The Old Man had quite a session with that redhead of yours before he packed me off as messenger boy.' He inspected Carrick with a feigned angelic innocence. 'One thing he didn't tell me was why you were out here with her in the first place.'

'She's not my redhead,' said Carrick patiently. 'And for the rest, would you believe me if I said we'd an idea about Broom?'

'No,' said Wills politely. 'Anyway, I've brought what you wanted.' He turned, waved an arm towards the stem, and Clapper Bell padded forward. The bo'sun was already wearing his black neoprene rubber skin-diving suit – a 'wet' suit, that admitted a thin film of water then used it as an insulator to retain body heat.

'All set, Clapper?' queried Carrick.

'Aye.' Bell contemplated the dark water, apparently delighted at the prospect ahead. 'Your stuff's laid out, sir.'

'Fine.' Carrick turned back to Jumbo Wills. 'We'll go down and have a look, fix a line to the car, then leave you to lead the other end ashore. The police can take care of hauling it out after that.'

Wills nodded. 'We've two coils of two-inch manilla, and a Mini shouldn't tip the scales at much over fourteen hundred pounds – they'll be more than enough.' He cleared his throat apologetically. 'Webb, I said I was messenger boy, and I meant it. The Old Man wants you to make sure there's nothing else lying around down there.'

'Like the obvious?' Carrick sighed and went back to get ready.

It didn't take long to dress in a twin of Bell's scuba suit, harness the two cylinders of the aqualung to his back, and go through the rest of the familiar drill which had long since become close to second nature. He was fastening the weight belt round his waist when Clapper Bell joined him again carrying a pair of sealed-beam lamps. Carrick took one, clipped it on, and nodded.

A moment later they stepped backwards together over the launch's side, hit the water with a single splash, and duck-dived down. Carrick led the way, the lamps blazing, thin trails of exhaled air bubbles rising from their outlet valves. The depth gauge on his wrist registered close on thirty feet when they reached bottom, then they finned along the line of the ledge until the lights picked out the sunken car.

The red Mini sat almost pathetically on all four wheels, as if parked ready for some undersea journey. A small fish darted away as Carrick opened the driver's door and inside he could see the ignition key was still in position. A suitcase lay across the rear seats. Working round to the rear, he arrived as Clapper Bell finally managed to open the trunk lid. A gout of trapped air burst loose in a giant bubble, and the lamps shone on a jumble of fishing gear.

They made two trips to the surface to bring down the manilla lines, then, the ropes heavy and clumsy under water, sweated within their suits as they carried out the awkward, time-consuming task of securing the ends to the car. When it was done, they went up again briefly to check that Jumbo Wills had the launch crew man-handling the other ends of the lines to the shore then sank down once more and began their exploration of the cove.

The twin cylinders on their backs were standard eighteen hundred p.s.i. jobs which meant, with the use demanded in the cove's depth, enough air for roughly another half-hour. Carrick had switched to his reserve valve's scanty allowance before, at last, they surfaced again at the launch. He followed Clapper Bell slowly up the diving ladder, shoved back his face mask, and took a thankful draw on the lit cigarette a hand placed between his lips.

'Any luck?' queried a voice.

He shook his head, swallowed to clear the dullness in his ears, and said wearily, 'None, but I suppose we've made somebody happier.'

'Blame the Navy, not me,' said the voice mildly. Carrick looked up and saw Superintendent Neilson standing over him. The policeman had a raincoat buttoned up to his neck and was shivering a little in the night air. He helped Carrick wriggle from the aqualung harness and inspected it with interest. 'Always wanted to try one of these. Still –' he shrugged. 'I've a mobile crane on its way by road from Oban to take care of the Mini, and I've seen the girl, of course – she's got a good mind, no frills, no time-wasting.' The thin fingers played thoughtfully with the scuba's harness clips. 'There's a bunch playing some game the hard way, Carrick – that's one thing we've got to accept now. What's worrying me more by the minute is the reason for it all.'

'I've no bright ideas, unless Captain Penman's ruddy torpedo is the answer,' said Carrick, moving along the launch with the policeman following.

'That?' Neilson winced at the thought then called over his shoulder. 'Gregor –'

'Yes – coming, sir.' The Borland constable, a craggily built young man, scrambled aboard from the ledge and came towards them. He glanced at Carrick with restrained interest then turned to Neilson. 'Sir?'

'Get on the car radio and make sure County Control have laid on that escort for the crane. I want it here double-quick.'

Gregor nodded and headed ashore again.

'No sense in roadblocks for that trailer, I'm afraid,' said Neilson apologetically. 'Not with the time lapse involved – it could be anywhere by now.' He hesitated and suggested hopefully, 'Like to make a guess at the kind of boat that was waiting out there?'

'Only that it was fairly small, probably no bigger than a drifter.' Carrick reached the hatchcover where Clapper Bell was already peeling out of his suit, began doing the same, and waited for Neilson's reaction.

'Well, there's no boat missing from the Borland contest fleet. We've checked.' Neilson tossed him a towel and went on. 'I've had the preliminary p.m. report on Broom. It's straightforward enough – cause of death, strangulation, though there was bruising at the back of his head, which makes it look as though he was unconscious when it happened. Time of death probably around three a.m., although they can't be too precise because of the water effect on temperature.'

'It still means he was probably alive about an hour after the attempt to get into *Starglow*,' reminded Carrick.

'Probably.' Neilson growled a qualified agreement. 'The fingerprint boys are on *Starglow* now, and MacNaught's working on a report of a dinghy that

86

was found tied to the wrong part of Borland jetty this morning.' He brightened a little. 'Still, we may strike it lucky when we get Broom's car up – and there's always a chance we might get a line on tonight's boat business.'

For Carrick's money, the latter was fragile hope. Within two hours' sailing of the cove there were probably half a hundred places where a boat could lie hidden, even without considering the islands beyond. The boat-trailer would be equally easy to tuck away. There was the old, apocryphal story of the army exercise in those same hills and moors, and of the field gun, left camouflaged one night, which couldn't be found till the following spring. But he restricted himself to a nod.

Eventually, Neilson went back to where his car was waiting. Minutes later, Jumbo Wills gave the order to cast off and the launch nosed its way out of the cove, her task completed. Carrick let the second mate handle things and was content to stay by the stern with Clapper Bell.

His back propped against the stern thwarts, the burly Glasgow-Irishman was soon snoring. Carrick stayed awake, listening to the almost hypnotic purr of the launch and the creaking of its hull.

Neilson was right. There had to be a considerable reason for it all. Yet the Navy's torpedo was too pat, too obvious an explanation. He was still trying to come up with some more sensible possibility when, at last, the launch reached home.

The blast, when it came, sounded like the crack of doom. It bellowed across Loch Rachan, echoed back from the hills, and started three crofters suing for pregnant cows frightened into premature labour.

Aboard *Marlin*, crockery rattled in the galley, the chief engineer cut himself shaving, and the picture of the Queen crashed from its place in the P.O.'s mess. Webb Carrick jerked awake from an odd nightmare about a torpedo which kept changing into a redhead, sat bolt upright in his bunk, and promptly banged his head on the ventilator trunking above.

Swearing, he rolled out of the bunk and scrambled over to the porthole, wondering if he was really hearing cries for help. Then, as he looked out, he relaxed and the curses took on a tone of wry indignation.

The Loch Rachan deep-sea angling festival was getting under way amid cheers from its competitors. A vast cloud of smoke was still rising from the muzzle of the small ceremonial cannon which the committee had used to signal the start from their headquarters ketch, and the first angling boats were already under way, heading out towards the Sound.

Carrick saw little reason for their crews to look so happy, even putting aside the eight a.m. start. Heavy grey clouds shaded most of the sky, there was already rain in the air, and the westerly wind was chopping the loch into a mosaic of broken, white-crested waves. But it took all kinds . . . He yawned, decided against burrowing back into the bunk, and began to dress. Halfway through he felt *Marlin*'s diesels start up and as he left his cabin in search of breakfast the fishery cruiser was already under way, moving at a sedate pace and following the last of the angling boats out of the loch.

The wardroom coffee, black and hot as melted pitch, burned the last of the sleep from his mind and he went up to the bridge feeling fairly close to normal.

"Morning, mister.' Captain Shannon, perched in the command chair, rasped a welcome then leaned forward to tap the helmsman on the shoulder. 'Harrison,

you're not handling a blasted bus. Nurse her, man –
like she was your wife, your sweetheart or whatever
you've got back home.'

'Aye, aye, sir.' Harrison kept his gaze ahead, his
naturally long face tightening a little. Carrick felt
mildly sympathetic. *Marlin*'s shallow draught, ideal
for her role and combined with an ability to execute
a full-rudder turn in an amazingly short length, could
make her a temperamental vessel to handle. And
now they were out in the Sound, in open water, the
heavier seas were already giving her the beginnings
of a roll.

'Well now, Mr Carrick –' Shannon leaned back,
scratching gently at his beard. 'I'd planned to let you
sleep for a little longer, but there's little need to ask
what wakened you. That damned popgun, eh?' He
chuckled to himself. 'Harrison, we'll be in the chartroom. Shout if you need me.'

He slid down from the chair and Carrick followed
him to the partitioned-off cubbyhole, where the
large-scale chart of the Sound was already spread on
the table. *Marlin*'s captain wasted no time in getting
down to business.

'We'll repeat yesterday's patrol pattern, with a particular emphasis on the exercise area boundaries.'
Hands in his pockets, he scowled down at the printed
sheet. 'Seems the talk after yesterday's practices was
that some of the best marks outside the exercise area
have been cleaned out by commercial boats.'

Carrick raised an eyebrow. 'So some of them may
try trespassing, sir?'

'The temptation's there,' agreed Shannon in a voice
which showed what he thought of the whole affair.
'We can't be everywhere at once, but we'll do the
next best thing. The Lighthouse Commission has
agreed we can put an officer on Whip Light for a few

days – I'm detailing young Wills, and he'll take his own R.T. link.'

A glance at the chart showed how much it made sense. One man with binoculars stationed in the lighthouse tower could observe a vast sweep of the southern Sound, ready to contact *Marlin* if he sighted any wandering strays. The lighthouse keepers couldn't be asked to handle that kind of job – quite apart from the fact that they had their own regular chores it would have been against normal Lighthouse Commission policy. The Commissioners, settled in their snug offices in Edinburgh, preferred to stay aloof from such matters. They concentrated on keeping their lights burning and their noses clean.

'Whip Light know about it, sir?'

'They should,' nodded Shannon. 'They were to be advised. Webb –' the first name term, as usual, put Carrick on his guard – 'go over with him and – ah – see him settled in. That'll give you a chance to have a word with the Leslie girl's father.'

'About the girl?' Carrick blinked.

'No.' Shannon's mouth twisted briefly. 'You're probably better informed than most on that subject. Find out if he's had any unusual night traffic recently. If there are boats sailing these waters without lights then it rates as very much our business – even Neilson can't deny that.'

'I see.' Carrick stayed straight-faced. 'Has the superintendent been objecting about us?'

'A little.' Shannon growled at the memory. 'Seems to think the Leslie girl should have come to him direct last night. He was on board about dawn to make the point.'

'Have they made any progress?' queried Carrick.

'Damned little. His fingerprint people were "analysing findings" and they'd got Broom's car ashore

90

intact.' He drummed briefly on the chart. 'Incidentally, the Navy are drafting in another two coastal minesweepers to look for that torpedo. If –' he laid a subtle emphasis on the word – 'if it's still there.'

'After last night you mean, sir?' Carrick found it hard to deny the possibility.

'Maybe.' Shannon touched his nose in wise fashion. 'Let's wait and see, mister – let's just wait and see.'

A drizzle of rain swept in as *Marlin* settled to her patrol routine, but soon gave way to scattered showers. Working the same steady W pattern, they met up with angling boats in sufficient number to show that Shannon had been right in fearing the competitors' tendencies were to keep to the south. But the *Anna B.*, top of Carrick's private trouble list, somewhat surprisingly well behaved, was working an old wreck site near Brosdile Island, far from the boundary line. *Marlin* passed the drifter close in, near enough to see the oilskin clad anglers standing patiently at her rail. Skinner Jones appeared briefly from the boat's wheelhouse, regarded the fishery cruiser with a scowl, then disappeared back into shelter.

Business picked up as soon as they reached the fringe of the exercise area. A converted lifeboat, two rods working from her stern, departed sadly northward at the fishery cruiser's warning. Five minutes later, in the middle of another rain squall, they repeated the process with an open twenty footer. And, almost inevitably, the first boat actually within the banned sector was the *Blue Vine*.

Scowling, Shannon took the electric loud-hailer from Carrick's hands as *Marlin* bore down on the drifter. His warning bellowed across the hundred yards of water between them, and Jenkins Batford's stocking-capped figure strode to the rail to reply.

'Och; we must have drifted a wee bit too much –'
The shout, through cupped hands, brought a dangerous purple to Shannon's face. The loud-hailer brayed
again, Batford waved, and the *Blue Vine* began to
retreat.

Marlin had had an audience. As the drifter headed
away, the long grey shape of an R class submarine
surfaced in leisurely fashion about a quarter mile
away. A signal light blinked from her conning tower.

Carrick grinned. 'She says, "Please keep your sheep
off our grass," sir.'

'Huh.' Shannon considered briefly, then thumbed
towards the bridge Aldis. 'Reply, mister. "Grass
appears worked from here. What species?"'

The R class's reply, when it came, was well outside
the signal manual. Shannon was delighted.

By ten-thirty a.m., two more boats shooed north,
Marlin had abandoned the W pattern and was heading down the Camas Dubh channel. At a steady
twenty-five knots, standing well out from the black
mainland cliffs and with a long, foaming wake churning from her stern, the fishery cruiser ate the distance
towards the growing finger of Whip Rock Lighthouse.
The sun had reappeared, and even the paintwork of
one of the centre channel radar buoys seemed to
sparkle as they passed its bobbing shape.

Jumbo Wills appeared on deck, laden under an
assortment of kit. He gazed unhappily towards the
tower of white masonry then, as Carrick joined him,
forced a smile.

'Well, I suppose it'll make a change,' he said deter-
minedly. 'And the job sounds easy enough.'

'As good as a holiday,' agreed Carrick, helping him
carry the bundles aft, where Clapper Bell had a couple
of deckhands standing ready by the duty launch. 'Just
don't go to sleep on it or the Old Man might leave
you there.'

The fishery cruiser cleared the channel, swung round in a curve until she was about five hundred yards west of the lighthouse, and the launch was lowered. The little craft bucked and pitched as she left the shelter of *Marlin*'s hull and spray was soon drenching along her length. Carrick could easily imagine that life on the lighthouse ahead was no picnic when the winter gales were at their height.

Eighty feet high and with a one million candle-power beam, Whip Rock was an impressive structure of massive, dovetailed granite blocks – three thousand tons of them in her structure, five years in the building back at the turn of the century. Her purpose was twofold, a guide to the channel beyond and a warning of the waiting tidal rocks which fanned around her base. There were plenty like her on the Scottish coast, each a monument to building work in time snatched between tides, to storm fury defied – fury like that recorded for one Hebridean light, where fourteen blocks of stone, each two tons in weight and set in cement almost forty feet above high water, had vanished in a single night of gale.

'Webb . . .' At his side Jumbo Wills wriggled uneasily as another curtain of spray swept across. 'Maybe I should have told the Old Man I've no head for heights.'

'Too late now,' said Carrick unsympathetically.

The seaman at the launch's helm had heard, and shook his head. 'The worst is if you're ill,' he said solemnly. 'I'd a cousin who was a keeper once. Took appendicitis, an' the weather too bad for anything to get near the light. Nearly dead he was before they managed to get a helicopter to lift him off.'

Jumbo Wills glared at him with something close to hate.

Nearer the lighthouse, within its hidden reef, things were easier. The launch edged gently alongside the small concrete landing place and one of the two men waiting to greet them secured its line then helped Carrick and Wills to climb up to their platform.

The older of the keepers, tall and lanky with a soft, friendly West Coast burr in his voice, held out his hand. 'Welcome to the Rock – I'm Dave Leslie, principal keeper. This is Danny Purvis.'

Carrick shook hands and carried out their side of the introductions. Alva Leslie's father was in his working rig of heavy sweater and serge trousers, a sun-tanned, freckled man with a thatch of hair almost as red as his daughter's.

'You'll find we're fairly comfortable,' he told Wills. 'Aye, we even got the television installed at the beginnin' of the year. Danny, take the second mate along and show him his quarters.'

The assistant keeper led Wills away and Dave Leslie eyed Carrick shrewdly. 'The Commissioners' radio call said you'd be wanting a word with me, Chief Officer.'

'We're interested in what you've maybe seen – or heard,' nodded Carrick.

'Right.' Leslie was unperturbed. 'We'll go up, then.'

Wills and his escort had already climbed the iron ladder to the entrance door some fifteen feet above the tower's platform. Carrick followed, ducked to avoid the pulley hoist above the doorway, and found himself at the bottom of a narrow, windowless access shaft with another long, almost vertical ladder leading upwards.

Leslie at his heels, he began the climb. At the top, the access shaft ended and he had a brief glimpse of a gleaming engineroom before Leslie guided him towards the start of the main stairway – winding, steeply angled, with metal treads and a brass handrail. They went up through another layer of engineroom, then a storeroom, Carrick glimpsed a set of neatly partitioned sleeping quarters on the fourth layer, and then, at last they'd emerged in the circular living room. The Whip Rock's third keeper, a small man with a taciturn face, was working by the kitchen area. He nodded briefly and returned to his task.

'Our Jimmy,' said Leslie apologetically. 'The quiet type. Now, just a step or two more.'

Carrick drew a deep breath and followed. This time the ladder led up through a quietly humming control room, with its great lamp pedestal and gearings. A few more rungs, and they were beside the giant glass prisms which surrounded the great bulb of the light, the windows on all sides shrouded in calico curtains to prevent the sun's rays damaging the precious lenses. Leslie opened a door, they stepped out, and he found himself looking down from a narrow, railed parapet to the rocks eighty feet below. *Marlin*'s launch looked like a toy moored at the landing stage, and all around the Sound of Jura was spread in panoramic glory.

'A fine view,' murmured Leslie. 'Your captain knows what he's doing.'

Still breathless, Carrick nodded. To the south-west, somewhere near the tip of Islay, a ship was a distant smoke-smudge on the horizon. The wind blew around them with a clothes-tugging impatience.

The lighthouse keeper eyed him tentatively. 'Mr Carrick, I'll start by thanking you for giving a helping hand to my girl.'

'Alva?' Carrick was dumbfounded. 'You've heard?'

'Aye. We've got the R.T. remember – and a man's family know the ropes.'

'Then you know about last night?'

The man's quick frown was answer enough. Carrick told him, and when he'd finished Leslie gripped the rail for a moment, staring down at the rocks.

'Damned if I like it,' he said finally. 'And now you're here wondering if I know anything about these boats, right?'

'Wondering – and hoping.'

Leslie rubbed a bony chin uncertainly. 'Well, there's been something without lights moving around the channel. One boat – aye, maybe two. The first time was about a week ago, an' they've been back a couple of times since. They might be the ones you're after, but they could have been drifters or line boats doing a spot o' fishing and trying to avoid people like you or the Navy.'

'Anything unusual in daylight?'

'Nope.' Leslie was firmly positive. 'Now your turn, Carrick. When you see her, tell that daughter o' mine to keep out of this trouble.' He shrugged. 'If they hadn't changed the contest dates for some damned fool reason about accommodation available, I'd be there myself to watch her. But as it is, remind her I'm still able to tan her backside.'

'I'll make sure she gets the message,' grinned Carrick. 'Dave, heard anything about a certain torpedo?'

'That thing?' Leslie growled at the thought. 'We've had Navy ships yo-yoing all over the place tryin' to find it. They've made the fish around here nervous wrecks.' He saw Carrick's puzzled amusement and explained. 'We've our own way with a line. Flying it off the balcony here on a kite, we can get a hook out well clear o' the rocks. That's by the way – come on, there should be some tea brewed.'

Chapter Five

A mug of tea, lighthouse fashion, is a thick, tarry brew in which flavour is sacrificed for strength and quantity ... an experience to be approached with care. Carrick finished his manfully, left Jumbo Wills busy unpacking the radio gear, and was escorted by Leslie back down the seemingly endless ladder rungs to the landing platform. The lanky keeper shook hands again as Carrick boarded the launch, then gave a final wave as it began buffeting a way out towards *Marlin*.

Minutes later, while the davit winches were still swinging the launch inboard, the fishery cruiser got under way, her diesels gathering speed. Carrick reached the deck, ordered the boat secured and turned to find Clapper Bell jog trotting towards him.

'Captain Shannon wants you straight away, sir,' said the bo'sun formally. One eyelid lowered in a fractional wink. 'He's frettin' about something. Chewed the steward a few minutes back, an' next thing tells me to have a boardin' detail ready.'

Carrick took the hint, headed for the bridge, and discovered Shannon hunched scowling in his command chair. The helmsman was standing stiffly by his post and Pettigrew, as watch officer, hovered discreetly in the background.

'Well, mister?' Shannon heard him in silence, then grunted, staring ahead. 'We'll talk about it later. That damned submarine's been complaining about more trespassers at the same position – came through on our wavelength and moaned about us not being there.' The audacity of the idea made him growl. 'Well, this time we'll teach whoever it is a lesson.'

'Board her, sir?'

Shannon nodded. 'Meantime, keep an eye on the radio room. Let me know when young Wills is operational from the light.'

Carrick was happy to oblige. The radio room made a comfortable haven, the operator, a cheerful character from the islands, talked happily about a blonde he'd met on the last leave while he flicked switches and tried to raise Jumbo Wills. Ten minutes later the loudspeaker was still yielding only background static when *Marlin*'s siren whooped out above their heads – a short-long-double-short signal, the order for another vessel to stop. Carrick abandoned the discussion, headed for the open deck, and found *Marlin* bearing down fast on their boundary-breaker.

For *Blue Vine*, which in theory they'd chased off miles to the north, it was second time unlucky. Barely under way in the swell, the drifter had several rods trolling from her stern – and on *Marlin*'s bridge Shannon stood out in the open by the canvas dodger, fists clenched, in imminent danger of explosion.

The siren whooped again and, reluctantly, the drifter hove to, her blunt nose coming round lazily to meet the swell. *Marlin*'s telegraph jangled and, in turn, the fishery cruiser slowed to come alongside. As they closed, Carrick saw that Jenkins Batford's passengers could have little to complain about – the *Blue Vine*'s deck was almost carpeted in a silver-grey collection of landed fish.

Batford appeared a moment later, standing by his wheelhouse. The drifter skipper grinned almost sheepishly as Shannon's voice barked through the loud-hailer.

'Batford, what the hell do you think you're doing?'

The stocking-capped figure spread his hands in a gesture of innocence and shouted back. 'There was a wee spot of engine trouble, captain – can I help it if we drifted this way again while it was bein' fixed?'

Marlin's loud-hailer spluttered then switched off.

'Mister Carrick –' Shannon beckoned angrily from above. 'Take three men, go aboard that – that tub, and sail her back to Borland. Tell that wool-topped idiot if he steps out of line once more I'll personally have his boat chopped from the competition fleet. Collect any others you find on the way.'

'Aye, aye, sir.' Carrick moved to join the three men Clapper Bell already had waiting by *Marlin*'s rail. The fishery cruiser edged closer, her fenders touched the old car tyres which did duty on the *Blue Vine*, and the little boarding party poised for an instant then dropped down to the fishing boat's swaying deck. The transfer accomplished, *Marlin*'s twin screws began churning and she surged away.

Carrick watched her go, with Captain Shannon still glaring from the bridge, then turned to inspect his charge. Jenkins Batford was making a leisurely, unflustered way towards him from the wheelhouse, stepping carefully round the fish piled on his deck.

'Eh . . . a fine day, Chief Officer,' greeted the skipper politely.

'For some,' agreed Carrick, glancing significantly at the *Blue Vine*'s haul. The anglers had reeled in their lines. The deck space around them was heavy with tope, pollack, at least a score of turbot, and the same number of large, gasping cod. Near the winch lay a wriggling sack of conger eels. 'Well, you know where you've got to head now.'

'Aye.' Batford made an effort to appear penitent. Then a twinkle broke through. 'Och, I'd say we'd done well enough, even though we'll lose the afternoon. No sense in being greedy.' He scratched his chin, slightly puzzled on one point. 'But what brought you back this way?'

'The Navy,' said Carrick. 'One of their submarines starting making worried noises.'

'So that's it!' Batford swore in indignation. 'Peepin' at us through a periscope – now what sort of fair play is that?'

'You can't be lucky all the time,' Carrick reminded him. 'What about your friend Skinner Jones? Any idea where he's hiding?'

'Friend?' Batford's nostrils flared a little at the word. 'I choose my friends carefully, Mr Carrick, and he's not among them. But if it's his boat you're meanin', she's still working that wreck mark to the west. Not that it'll do his folk much good.'

'At least they're staying out of trouble.' Carrick nudged him in the direction of the wheelhouse. 'Let's go.'

Engine thumping steadily, the *Blue Vine* began plugging north towards Loch Rachan. Soon Carrick collected another stray, this time a converted lifeboat with three sheepishly crestfallen competitors aboard. He ordered them to fall in astern, watched them obey, then the drifter continued on her way.

'Mind if I give a bit of help?' Batford, cheerfully resigned to his own position, seemed to enter into the spirit of the game. 'If I was looking for a good mark around here, there's always in behind Garra Island.' He pointed through the salt-stained wheelhouse glass to the high-set stretch of grass-crowned rock growing a few points to starboard ahead. 'How about having a wee look, Chief Officer?'

'You –' Carrick didn't finish, took a long breath, then nodded. Batford's philosophy was practical enough. If he had to stop fishing then he didn't see why others should escape.

The drifter's wheel spun and she went in towards the little island with the converted lifeboat still trailing. They'd skirted most of Garra's eastern shore when Batford gave a sudden chuckle and pointed again.

'Now there's a surprise, eh?'

Carrick had his third stray – and this time it was *Starglow*. The slim-lined cabin launch, one rod working from her stern, was heaving gently in the swell close by the next headland.

'That lassie Alva should have known better,' mused Batford sanctimoniously. He glanced slyly at Carrick. 'Mind you, I thought I recognized the boat when we came down this way. Eh . . . maybe you'll want to deal with this one personally, Mr Carrick?'

Carrick sighed and grinned ruefully despite himself. 'Maybe I'd better,' he agreed. 'But you're still on course for Loch Rachan, and I'll be right behind you.'

'Can I do anything else with three of your men aboard?' Batford, eyes still twinkling, reached for the throttle lever.

Starglow's occupants showed varying degrees of interest as the *Blue Vine* was brought skilfully alongside their craft. Carrick timed his jump across the heaving gap, landed in a half-crouch on the cabin launch's deck, and drew himself upright as Page Abbott came towards him from the stern.

'Something wrong, Carrick?' demanded *Starglow*'s owner. He seemed nervous and moistened his lips. 'If it's where we're fishing –'

Carrick nodded. Behind them, he could see Douglas Swanson's red face peering with a worried interest from the cockpit's bridge. Marge Harding was there too, wrapped in a quilted anorak jacket over thick wool ski-pants, clinging to a rail with one hand and frowning.

'You're about a mile inside the prohibited area, Mr Abbott.' Out of the corner of his eye he saw the *Blue Vine* beginning to draw away and silently cursed Jenkins Batford. 'I'm under orders to collect any craft over the boundary line and shepherd them back to Loch Rachan.'

'Well, maybe we have been a little bit naughty.' Some of the tension seemed to drain from Abbott. He turned round and raised his voice. 'We're over the line, Marge. Fishery Protection are shovelling us back to Borland.'

'Good.' Her voice held a tightly controlled edge. 'I wish they'd come sooner.'

'Hardly matters anyway,' growled Abbott, facing Carrick again. 'I haven't got into a decent fish all morning. What do we do?' He nodded towards the two boats, now clearing the headland. 'Want us to play follow my leader home?'

'Yes.' Puzzled, Carrick looked around. 'I thought Alva would have kept you clear of the exercise area.'

'Don't blame her.' Abbott signalled to Swanson and pointed towards the boats ahead. As *Starglow*'s engines quickened he looked at Carrick strangely. 'You mean you haven't heard?'

'About what?'

'Well, that she couldn't come –'

At the stern, Abbott's reel gave a sudden scream and line began whipping out. The man's pale face lit like a beacon and he dived aft, Carrick following, watching as he slid into the fishing chair and grabbed the rod. It was an expensively old-fashioned seven foot split cane, handmade, an expert's tool, the kind seldom seen in the face of modern competition from cheaper steel tube and glass fibre.

'Now look, Mr Abbott –'

'In a minute. I'm into something – and it's big!' Abbott ignored him, concentrated on the rod, gained a little slack, then frowned and next moment bellowed over his shoulder to Swanson.

'Cut 'em!'

Starglow's engines died, Abbott pumped vigorously on the line then swore excitedly as the strain from below suddenly solidified and the rod bent like a tightly strung bow.

'Bottomed – it's a ruddy skate and a big one.' He glanced pleadingly at Carrick. 'Look, it's the first decent thing I've had on. We can wait a few minutes, can't we?'

It was likely to be more than a few, but Carrick nodded impatiently. 'All right, but what about the girl?'

'That?' Abbott frowned at the distraction and glanced over his shoulder towards the cockpit. 'Marge, tell him about the girl –'

Marge Harding stirred from her position and came along the swaying deck towards them, never letting go of the launch's rail. 'Our little redhead, Mr Carrick?' She shrugged, showing little interest. 'Well, she came down to the jetty this morning and met us, then that detective Neilson, the one who came round bothering us about fingerprints, arrived and marched her off.'

'Did he say why?' demanded Carrick.

'Not in so many words.' Her lips puckered cynic- ally. 'He made noises about her "giving further assist- ance". But I can guess – I'd say she's in trouble up to her freckled little neck.'

With a growl, Carrick swung round again to Abbott. The man had momentarily slackened his line and was busily attaching a lead weight to the nylon on a running clip. 'Abbott, do you know anything more about this?'

'Me? No –' Temporarily oblivious to anything else around, Abbott tightened the line again and let the weight slide free. It raced down the nylon and disappeared into the swell. Down below, if Abbott's guess was right, the skate had settled into the bottom mud and was using the powerful suction of its enormous body wings to hold fast. But in a moment it was going to be rudely thumped on the nose.

'Now –' Abbott felt a quiver reach the rod, an indefinable slackening, and pumped triumphantly. The reel wound line with a scream of gears, the muscles on his deceptively thin wrists knotted like cords as he fought the fish up from the deep. Then, suddenly, he cursed. The line had gone slack, the tension was off the rod, the fish was free. In a few seconds the last of the line was cranked up and he scowled bitterly at the broken trace.

'Hard luck.' Carrick observed the conventions, but with little sympathy.

'Next time I'll use heavier tackle,' promised Abbott, still scowling.

'But not here.' Marge Harding clutched the anorak tighter at her throat, almost savouring the situation. 'If you do, the Fishery Protection boys clap you straight in the pokey. Right, Mr Carrick?'

'More or less,' nodded Carrick. The *Blue Vine* and her other unwilling consort were out of sight, and time had acquired a fresh importance. 'Let's get moving.'

'Why not?' grunted the launch owner. 'After that I've had enough for one day.' He nodded to Swanson in the cockpit and twirled one hand above his head. Swanson waved, *Starglow*'s engines came to life and the launch began to gather way.

* * *

They reached Loch Rachan under an overcast sky with low cloud misting the hills, and found the Borland jetty and its surrounding mooring buoys almost deserted. Only the big committee ketch and a couple of smaller boats were in sight, and Swanson brought the launch straight in, coming alongside the jetty in a flamboyant display of throttle control.

Carrick clambered up on to the planked walk, took the line Abbott tossed him, and tied it to a bollard. As he turned to leave, a tweed-clad local with an arm-band marked 'Official' came hurrying along from the shore.

'Trouble, Chief Officer?' he asked anxiously.

'Just a stray,' said Carrick briefly. He nodded towards the mouth of the loch. 'You'll have another two in soon – we passed them about four miles back.'

'Over the boundary, eh?' The committee man bristled with sudden authority. 'I'll deal with them, don't worry.'

'Have fun,' said Carrick absently. He left the man heading purposefully towards *Starglow* and started off towards the village.

Borland's police station, like most one-man posts on the West Highland coast, was a small, modern cottage split equally into living quarters for the constable's family and office proper. It lay at the end of a lane behind the local ex-Service Club hall, surrounded by a small neatly cultivated garden which had the in-evitable official noticeboard planted firmly in the middle of the front lawn.

Carrick squeezed past the pram with sleeping infant which blocked most of the narrow path leading to the front door, pushed the door open, and found himself up against a small wooden counter.

'Sorry, Constable Gregor's out –' Detective Sergeant MacNaught stuck his head round an inner door, broke

105

off with a friendly grin, and relaxed a little. 'Come on through, Carrick.'

He lifted the counter lid, passed through, and followed the detective into the other room. It was furnished with a desk, two chairs, a telephone and a filing cabinet and most of the polished wood floor-space was covered by a selection of sodden clothing.

'Broom's?'

'Aye.' MacNaught picked up a shirt and tossed it to one side. 'Just givin' them another going over. If you're looking for the superintendent, he's due back in a minute.'

'Good.' Carrick leaned back against the doorpost and eyed the sergeant thoughtfully. 'I hear Neilson grabbed Alva Leslie this morning.'

'Grabbed?' MacNaught's black eyebrows almost touched as they rose in amusement. 'Led her gently by the arm is nearer it, man. Grab that girl an' I reckon you'd get your face clawed in double-quick time. But we've let her go again, for the moment anyway.'

'What's it all about?' Carrick fished out his cigarettes, offered the pack, then, as the sergeant shook his head, lit one for himself. 'I thought you were satisfied with her story.'

'We were,' agreed MacNaught cautiously. 'But there are some puzzles now – new puzzles, if you like it better. Broom's car, for a start. He arrived in Borland early on Sunday, had it serviced in the village garage, an' the mechanic took the usual note o' the speedo mileage. He's supposed to have been around here all the time after that, yet there's a hundred miles more on the clock since then.'

'So?'

'So we're curious,' said a mildly amused voice behind Carrick. He looked round, then nodded as Superintendent Neilson entered the room. Neilson tossed his hat on the desk, loosened his coat, and

106

added, 'What's more interesting, and this time involving the girl, is that we've two witnesses, fishermen, who swear they saw her being rowed back to the *Starglow* that night around midnight – despite the fact she still says she didn't leave the boat.'

'Local men?' queried Carrick, frowning.

'No. From that drifter the *Anna B.*' Neilson saw the look on his face and wagged an admonitory finger. 'All right, you've a quarrel with Skinner Jones and his crew. But that's no business of mine, Carrick – and I don't want witnesses being pressured, understood?'

'Understood,' said Carrick softly. 'But one way or another somebody has to be lying.' He drew gently on his cigarette then let the smoke trickle out. 'Incidentally, you know that Abbott and his friends were out in a hired car last night?'

'I've seen it,' grunted Sergeant MacNaught. 'An old Ford wi' no spotlight or towbar. It wasn't the one pulling that boat-trailer, that's for sure.'

'Anyway, there's not even a hint that Abbott is involved. He seems a solid enough citizen as far as I can make out,' protested Neilson. He propped his lean length against the edge of the desk and gestured placatingly. 'Look, Carrick, I've no particular reason to say Alva Leslie is either, come to that – damn it, she took you to the cove last night. But I've got to try to be sure of everything and everyone.'

'Where is she now?'

'At the Dairg Tower – or she was a few minutes back. I went round to have another talk with Peter Mack, which was a waste of time.' Neilson grimaced at the recollection 'So far we've managed to keep the press mob out of this, but if they turn up I won't have to guess twice about who tipped them off. He's already begun talking about murder being a tourist attraction.'

'Nasty, but he's probably right.' Carrick was ready to leave, but he stayed where he was as the telephone began ringing. Neilson sighed and scooped up the receiver.

'Borland police –' He listened and showed a slight surprise. 'Yes, you're speaking to him. What's the message?' Lips clamped together, he heard the caller out in silence, glanced once in Carrick's direction, then finally muttered an acknowledgement and hung up.

'Submarine flotilla H.Q., Gareloch,' he said glumly. 'Captain Penman will be here at two and wants an immediate meeting. Seems he's also radioing *Marlin* – he wants Shannon to be in on it.'

'Sounds like a minor panic,' murmured Carrick. 'Any hint what it's about?'

'From the Navy?' Neilson snorted. 'For all I know, somebody's stolen a submarine.' Then he looked quickly from one man to the other and shook his head hopefully. 'It couldn't happen – could it?'

The baby in the pram was making a gathering, hungry-sounding protest as Webb Carrick walked down the police cottage path. He stopped, clucked at it sympathetically, was rewarded by a startled howl, and beat an immediate retreat, hoping for Neilson's sake that the constable's wife was at home.

His target was the Dairg Tower, but on the way he checked the scene at the jetty. *Blue Vine* and the converted lifeboat had joined *Starglow*. Another boat, still too far out to be identified, was coming up the loch towards the moorings – probably the latest addition to *Marlin*'s tally of collected boundary-breakers.

At the hotel, the entrance foyer was deserted though a clatter of crockery from the dining room's direction showed someone, at any rate, was preparing for a later invasion. He heard a murmur of voices, traced the sound to the cashier's office, found the door ajar, and looked in.

'Well, see who's here,' said Alva Leslie grimly. She was perched on the edge of the office desk, her back to the window. 'I told you he'd be next, didn't I, Jean?'

The dark-haired receptionist smiled ruefully in his direction from the other side of the desk and shook her head. 'Give the man a chance, Alva. It's not his fault.'

'Did I say it was?' Alva Leslie pursed her lips.

'Hold on,' protested Carrick, bewildered. 'What isn't my fault?'

Jean MacDonald chuckled and shook her head. 'Don't try and involve me, Mr Carrick. I've enough problems of my own.' She gathered up some papers from the desk and headed for the door. 'But I'll say this – I think Alva's had a raw deal.'

Carrick waited until she had gone out, leaving the door almost closed, then crossed towards the desk. 'Well?'

Alva shrugged her general disgust. 'I've just had the Harding woman tell me that I'm no longer required on *Starglow* – in short, I've been kicked out.' She mimicked bitterly. 'After all, my dear, you can hardly call yourself available when the police are taking such an active interest in your affairs. Whether you went rowing with someone that night is your business of course, but Mr Abbott feels – '

'Hold on.' Carrick frowned and cut her short. 'I've heard about this from Neilson –'

'And it's a pack of lies.' She came down from the desk and faced him indignantly, brown eyes sparkling their anger. 'That bunch on the *Anna B*. –'

'All right,' he soothed her. 'But how would Abbott know the story?'

Alva shrugged. 'Does it matter? I've been kicked out, that's all I know.'

Carrick rubbed his chin, deciding that Sergeant MacNaught had been right. This particular redhead didn't take kindly to being pushed around. 'Well, it probably didn't help that I caught them working a mark off Garra Island and booted them back here.'

'A mark off Garra?' It was her turn to look bewildered 'Well, I certainly didn't suggest it – there's nothing much around that place, never has been.'

'You're sure?' Carrick glanced idly towards the door and froze a little. The light from the hallway beyond was streaming in through the narrow gap where it had been left ajar and a clear shadow was being thrown on the office wall. He put a finger to his lips then pointed and said loudly, 'Well, Abbott got into something big, though he lost it.'

Her eyes had widened, but she nodded and took her cue. 'Well, I can't know all the marks, of course –'

Carrick took two swift strides to the door, grabbed the handle, and yanked it open. The small, kilted figure of Peter Mack practically tumbled into the room.

'Looking for someone?' asked Carrick sardonically.

The hotelier gulped, his fat face drained of colour. 'I – I heard voices,' he said lamely. 'I thought –'

'That you'd listen for a spell?' asked Alva with a bright innocence.

'No – no, of course not.' Mack squirmed under their gaze. 'I – well, I just don't like barging in on people.' He swallowed again and tried to bluster on. 'Anyway, I'm glad I found you, Carrick.'

'Why?'

'Because – ah – as festival secretary I'm dealing with the boats who broke the boundary regulations.' The man regained confidence and the words came hurrying out. 'The committee has decided each rod involved will be penalized on a pointage basis equal to twenty per cent of the poundage of fish he caught.'

'I'd watch it, Mr Mack,' said Alva with a mock concern. 'You're liable to be carved up for bait when they find out.'

'It – well, it has to be done.' Mack moistened his lips. 'I thought you'd want to know, Carrick . . .' His voice died away and he backed towards the door. A faint, awkward nod of his head, and he was gone.

As the door closed, the girl laughed aloud. 'That's something which was long overdue.' She raised an eyebrow at the frown on Carrick's face. 'What's wrong? He's the keyhole type, but he didn't hear anything that mattered.'

'Probably not.' Carrick relaxed, but still wished he could have been equally sure. 'Anyway, let's move out – he might find the temptation too strong and try again.'

They left the room. The hotel foyer was still deserted, and Alva went over to the reception desk. She collected a long, one-piece glass fibre rod propped behind it then dragged a canvas haversack into view.

'I'll take that.' Carrick took the haversack by its strap and whistled at the weight. 'What's in this?'

'Just the rest of my fishing gear.'

'There's enough of it.' He shouldered the haversack, went on ahead to open the main door and, once she'd manoeuvred the rod's length out into the open, followed her down the steps to the gravelled pathway. 'I saw your father this morning.'

'Out at the light?' She swung round, surprised, and the rod's tip whipped the blooms from a solitary rosebush.

'Uh-huh. We're using it as a sentry-box.' Carrick inspected her with a grin. 'He said I was to tell you to stay out of any more trouble or he'd –'

111

'Tan my backside – I know.' There was warm affection in her voice. 'I managed to wangle a radio call to him a couple of nights back.'

'He told me,' nodded Carrick. 'Alva, did you know they've heard a boat nosing around at night?'

Her mouth tightened and she shook her head. 'No, he didn't mention it. Down there, up here – somebody's being busy, whatever the reason.'

They walked on, and she looked wistfully towards the boats moored in the loch. 'I think I'll try the *Blue Vine*, Webb. Jenkins Batford might take me on for tomorrow's session.'

'In Broom's place?' Carrick scuffed a loose pebble along the ground. 'Probably, if you can pay.'

'Just and no more.' She stopped, let the rod trail, and gripped it by the butt. 'Let's see what my bank vault says.' One hand gripped the butt, the other twisted hard on the cork plug at its base. The plug turned and came free, and she slipped her fingers into the hollow socket exposed. When she drew them out, a thin wad of folded notes came free. She thumbed them quickly and was satisfied. 'The *Blue Vine* it is, and hang the expense.'

Carrick stared at the butt, the faint beginning of a possibility stirring in his mind. 'Alva, how many rods are like that?'

'The hollow butt?' She pondered for a moment. 'Quite a lot of the new glass fibre models and a few of the alloy tube types. Why?'

'I'm wondering if anyone checked Broom's rod.' Carrick shoved his hat a little way back on his head, his manner thoughtful. 'Alva, there's a couple of things you could do with less fuss than if I started asking. I want to know how many miles Page Abbott clocked up on that car he hired last night. The other one might interest you even more. Ask around if

112

Abbott or his friends have had any contact with the *Anna B.'*

'Meaning they might have rigged this story about me so they had an excuse to kick me off *Starglow*?' She showed wry understanding, put the money back in its hiding place, and rammed the plug home. 'Planning a special kind of fishing expedition, Webb?'

'Maybe. But there's no mark to work yet – just a hunch,' he warned.

She looked at him for a moment, nodded, then took the haversack.

Detective Superintendent Neilson had a cigarette dangling unlit between his lips when Carrick returned to the police cottage, and his reaction to the request was a faint stir of amusement.

'Broom's angling gear?' He went over to the wall behind the counter, unhooked a key from a collection on a nail, and tossed it over. 'The stuff's still in the car round the back. Help yourself.' Then, as a cautious afterthought, he glanced at his sergeant. 'Better show him the way.'

The Borland constable's garage was a simple wooden affair. Carrick turned the key in the lock, swung open the doors, and the daylight poured in on the little red Mini he'd last seen at the bottom of the cove. The rough concrete floor of the garage was stained black with the water still dripping from the car, and the boot lid lay open.

'Superintendent checked it himself,' said Sergeant MacNaught laconically, propping himself against the door. 'But go ahead, Carrick.'

Broom's rod was a sectional job, three sections of alloy tube with steel ferrule joins. Conscious of MacNaught's open disinterest, he picked up the butt section and examined the base. It was a different type from Alva's, a brass plug with a cork insert, but when he twisted it it gave easily, turning on a broad thread. A shadow fell across the car and he turned to find MacNaught standing bear-like at his side. Lips pursed, the detective watched as he finished unscrewing the plug and poked a finger into the hollow socket.

'Anything?'

Carrick nodded and coaxed out a single sheet of folded paper. It was still dry, and he spread it out with an eager care – then felt a sudden disappointment. The paper had only two roughly pencilled triangles on its surface. They shared the same base line, had one base angle in common, and one was really only an extension of the other. And as far as he was concerned they meant absolutely nothing. The other side of the sheet was blank.

MacNaught scratched his chin. 'What the hell's it supposed to be?' he asked plaintively.

A few minutes later, scowling at the paper on the desk of his temporary office, Neilson said much the same thing for about the tenth time. He glared at Carrick and his sergeant as if holding them personally responsible for the lack of an answer.

'Man, you must have had more than just a vague idea there was something in there,' he grumbled. 'Can't you make some kind of sense from it?'

'No.' Carrick stood over at the window, looking out at the loch. *Marlin* had arrived, which meant Captain Shannon would be on his way. But there was still no sign of Captain Penman. 'I told you – it could make sense that Nathan Broom spotted this bunch when he was fishing around Silver Cove, found out something about them, but decided to stay quiet for a spell. Maybe he hid this away just before he was attacked, maybe he put it in the rod as a kind of insurance –'

'Or maybe it has nothing to do with anything but this ruddy angling fiesta.' Neilson sighed and chewed his lip. 'Why couldn't these damned triangles be some kind of pattern he wanted the *Blue Vine* to try out over a collection of blasted fishing marks?'

'It's possible.' Try as he might, Carrick was equally lost.

The door opened, Constable Gregor looked round, cleared his throat, and a moment later Captain Shannon stumped into the room. He grunted a general greeting, then glanced at his watch.

'Two o'clock – where's Penman?'

'Don't ask me –' began Neilson, then stopped, a strangely querulous expression on his face. A distinctive, chopping engine-beat was approaching, gathering volume fast. A moment later the helicopter, a little Westland Wasp with Navy insignia on its distinctive yellow tail section, came into their view through the window.

Losing height steadily, the Wasp seemed headed straight for the cottage roof then, as the beat of its rotors filled the room, it vanished overhead a scant fifty feet up. In the station living quarters, Constable Gregor's infant began howling.

Neilson swallowed hard as the Wasp's noise died. 'I think we can take it Penman's arrived,' he said heavily. 'There's a field just behind here.' He glanced at MacNaught as the baby's howls continued. 'Tell Gregor we – ah – don't blame the child, but we'd be glad if he could silence it.'

MacNaught grinned and went out. In a matter of seconds, the howling stopped – Carrick hated to imagine just how the harassed Gregor had achieved the miracle. And when MacNaught returned he brought with him the immaculately uniformed Captain Penman. The Gareloch Flotilla administration and security officer had a hide briefcase under one arm and his face bore the look of a man consciously carrying more than his share of troubles.

'Well, gentlemen –' he nodded briefly round the room – 'I see we're all here.'

'Now, at any rate,' grunted Shannon.

The Navy man didn't rise to the bait, a sign in itself. He fumbled with the briefcase while MacNaught found extra chairs then, once they were seated around the desk, gazed at them again with eyes which showed something close to despondency through their thick spectacle lenses.

'I've kept in touch with what's been happening here,' he began carefully, the briefcase propped open on his lap. 'The urgency about this meeting is because something has happened which – well, demands every possible priority.'

Neilson raised an eyebrow but said nothing. They watched while Penman reached into the briefcase and took out a single sheet of paper.

'This is a photostat of a letter received by Flag Officer, Scotland.' Penman twitched a little at the mentioning of that Olympian individual. 'It was delivered by post this morning and it offers the return of our torpedo on payment of what it describes as a "suitable reward".'

Carrick's low whistle matched the others' reaction. 'How much?'

'Ten thousand pounds in used notes.' Penman's voice quivered at the final indignity. 'If we accept, we've to put a one-line advert in the "Lost and Found" section of the *Oban Times* – the words "Mother is willing".'

'And is she?' Captain Shannon tried to bury a chuckle in his beard.

Penman glared at him. 'Do I have to spell it out, Shannon? Someone – probably one of your damned

116

fishermen – has found that torpedo. Now they're trying to blackmail us into paying for its return –'

'If they've actually got it,' murmured Neilson.

'They've got it,' grated Penman. 'This quotes serial
numbers and the rest.' He pushed the photostat across
the desk. 'See for yourself. The original was posted in
Glasgow at noon yesterday – the envelope and paper
could be bought anywhere, and our security people
say there's no other lead.'

Slowly, the photostat was passed round the group.
Neatly printed in ink capitals, the letter was short and
to the point.

SIR,

WE HAVE BEEN FORTUNATE IN FINDING
YOUR TORPEDO SERIAL 26 EX 1715YD (H) WITH
DUMMY WARHEAD NUMBER 26 EX 7Y. WE
WILL BE GLAD TO ARRANGE RETURN IF . . .

If ten thousand pounds was forked out first, a cool
three times the value of any ordinary torpedo.
Someone knew he'd got hold of an item considerably
out of the ordinary.

'Well?' demanded Penman, turning to Neilson.
'Does that give you a motive for murder, Superintendent – murder and the rest?'

'It could,' agreed Neilson reluctantly. 'Except – well,
even if Broom knew something about it, where does
this business of a prowler out on the loch fit in?'

'Does it have to?' Penman was impatient. 'Ask
Shannon who is most likely to find a runaway
torpedo.'

'And what do you pay them when they do?'
grunted Shannon. He saw the blank looks on the two
detectives' faces and glanced at Carrick. 'Tell them,
mister.'

'Well . . .' Carrick hesitated, while Penman flushed and rubbed the gold rings on his left cuff with the fingers of his right hand. This was always a touchy affair. 'There's a more or less fixed scale, but the payment can be as low as five pounds, sometimes ten. It only goes higher if there are special circumstances.'

The rewards and the rules were crazy. If they'd wanted, Carrick could have gone on to something crazier, what happened when a floating mine was discovered. Every so often one of those ancient, rusty, temperamental globes of lethal peril popped to the surface. Find it washed up on a beach, and you might get ten shillings. Find it at sea within two miles of shore and the reward went up to two pounds – a week's cigarette money. Locate it two miles out or more, and it was worth ten pounds. He'd heard at least one crazy tale of a boat finding a mine and risking towing it further out for the sake of the extra cash.

'I don't decide the payments,' protested Penman. 'Anyway, they're in line with what's paid by other NATO forces.'

'But you should be ashamed of them,' thundered Shannon, thumping the desk.

'At least there's no security risk in the normal sense, correct?' interrupted Neilson hastily. He didn't wait for an answer. 'Let's be thankful for that. Now here's something we –' he winced and corrected himself – 'I mean Chief Officer Carrick found in Broom's stuff.'

The folded paper from the rod butt was examined by each captain in turn with the same negative response.

'Pity.' Neilson lit a cigarette, took a long draw, and looked around hopefully. 'Well, any suggestions?'

There was a long silence in the room. At last, Carrick decided to speak what was on his mind.

118

'These boats operating without lights could mean the torpedo is still in the area, that it hasn't been moved yet.'

Penman jerked upright at the idea. 'Or they only know where the torpedo is lying, but haven't recovered it!' He whipped off his heavy spectacles and used them like a pointer. 'That could be it, Neilson.'

The detective pursed his lips. 'You mean this torpedo might be difficult to bring up?'

'Very difficult, depending on how it's lying.' Shannon's voice was dry, and for the moment he and Penman were welded in a common amazement at the landsman's ignorance. 'They might be able to get down to it, or it might be beached. Either way they could get these serial numbers yet still not have physical possession. Presuming the torpedo is still in the exercise area, then they've also got the risk of being spotted by some Navy craft while they're trying to lift it.'

'And flotilla manoeuvres continue for another ten days,' nodded Penman. 'Except for tonight – there's a complete break from dusk till dawn tomorrow.' He saw Shannon's interest and shrugged a little. 'Call it avoiding complications. There's a new oil drilling rig, the Nanda Group's *Sea Raven*, being towed round from one of the Clyde shipyards to the east coast and they're using the Camas Dubh channel. She's a slow hulk to drag, and the tugs want any shelter they can get. Anyway, if she used the ordinary open sea route it would add a lot of time to the journey.'

The two Fishery Protection men nodded their understanding. A floating rig platform, often the size of a football field, was a clumsy monster. And the North Sea oil and gas drilling bonanza off the British coast was fast reaching the stage where days, even hours saved mattered.

119

'Tonight?' Sergeant MacNaught sucked his ball-point pen and glanced at Neilson. 'How about the angling boats, sir – haven't they some kind of night-fishing session?'

Shannon answered. 'That's tomorrow, sergeant. But if any boat does go out she'll have plenty of time to get clear. These rigs are lit up like Christmas trees – you can spot them a mile away.'

'Even so, tonight might be worth special attention,' murmured Neilson. 'No Navy units in the area could be a temptation to our friends.' He had another matter on his mind. 'This letter to your top brass worries me, Penman. Posted in Glasgow yesterday – that's a two hundred mile round trip from Borland, if it was written here.'

'There's Broom's car –' began MacNaught.

'But the mileage wouldn't fit,' reminded Carrick. 'There's another car around, remember – the one with the boat-trailer.'

'Even so, we only know when the letter was posted,' growled Shannon. 'When it was written could be different. It could have gone from here by boat to a harbour nearer the city, then been given to someone at the other end to post later.' He pursed his lips. 'We might have a chance along that line. Most commercial boats working the Sound of Jura over the past week or so have been unloading their catch at Ayr. Penman, could that egg-beating contraption of yours take another passenger, Carrick, for instance?'

'Straight away,' agreed Penman enthusiastically. 'And we'll bring him back, of course.'

'Fine.' Shannon relaxed into his chair. 'You know what to do at Ayr, mister?'

Carrick nodded.

120

Chapter Six

The helicopter pilot was a young lieutenant with dark sunglasses, an Irish accent and a cheerful confidence. And he didn't believe in wasting time. Twenty minutes after takeoff from the field behind the police station the Westland Wasp touched down at Gareloch submarine base and Captain Penman disembarked. Then the Wasp climbed again, heading high above the wide blue spread of the Firth of Clyde, the islands and coastline below like so many blobs and splotches of spilled green paint. In roughly the same time again the rotors changed their note once more as the grey sprawl of the seaport town of Ayr began to grow ahead.

The lieutenant talked briefly into his helmet microphone, listened, acknowledged, then raised his voice a little as he turned to Carrick.

'Control say you'll be met at the airport. Okay?'

Carrick nodded as the helicopter swung and began to lose height. Prestwick international airport, a mile or so beyond the fringe of the town, was as good a place as any – and one where the Wasp's arrival could cause little fuss.

In a couple of minutes more the helicopter sank down to land on the fringe of the airport's terminal apron. As its rotors died and he climbed out of the little bubble cabin a small black saloon car was already purring towards them. He gave a wave of thanks to the lieutenant and hurried across. The car halted, he opened the passenger door, got in, and grinned his surprise at the driver.

'Well, who else did you expect?' demanded the man behind the wheel. 'The Easter Bunny or somebody? Old Shannon called me on R.T., and said he felt you needed someone responsible to hold your hand.'

'Then why choose you?' Carrick closed the door and relaxed back on the seat. Bill Duart, a burly individual of his own age, was one of the duty harbourmasters at Ayr. Ex-Navy, his reason for being ashore was a metal hook where his left hand had once been. 'You know the score, Bill?'

'Only a little.' Duart used his hook to flick the car's selector to Drive and they began to pull away. 'Shannon said you'd fill in the details.'

Carrick did, while they drove the long, straight road towards the town. Duart kept his eyes on the road but his interest was plain.

'Right,' he agreed as Carrick finished. 'I know the man you want to see. But not in that uniform, or every boat on the coast will know about it by dusk.' The hook waved towards the back. 'There's a spare raincoat on the floor. Better put it on, and leave that cap behind.'

He struggled into the coat as the car crossed the bridge over the River Ayr and, turn indicator winking, swung right towards the harbour. Duart drew it in at one of the quayside parking lots, switched off, and they got out.

The harbour was compact but busy. Across the water, a bulk carrier was loading coal, a dockside crane picking up railway wagon after railway wagon of the black dirt and upending each in turn so that its contents torrented down into the waiting maw of its hold. On their side, the first stretch of quay was occupied by a mass of tied-up pleasure craft and immediately below them lay the start of the fishing fleet. Drifters and motor fishers big and small were tied three deep at the quay's edge, a noisy bustle of swinging booms landing unending baskets of fish, of ice being loaded, of fish-scaled decks being hosed down.

The fish market building, a long, large, single-storey structure with open sides and neon strip lighting, lay further down, immediately beside the quay. In the scanty space between another bustle of porters and driftermen were boxing the fish as they came ashore, weighing the boxes, stacking them on trolleys, then wheeling them into the market building where each boat's catch was displayed in a separate row.

'Watch your feet,' warned Duart, leading the way along the quayside where the stonework was already coated in a high-smelling mixture of fish slime, silver scales and melting ice mash. Carrick followed and they entered the building, where the noise immediately multiplied in volume.

'Wait here –' Duart elbowed him towards a pillar, winked, and walked off. Carrick lit a cigarette and looked around, seeing several faces he recognized but trusting on them being too busily involved to notice him in turn. Two auctioneers were already at work near the top of the hall, each surrounded by a knot of agents and wholesalers, their sing-song chanting indecipherable to an outsider as the bidding progressed. As a sale was made, it brought nothing more emphatic than a sudden grunt from the auctioneer concerned as he strode on to the next catch. Behind him, porters immediately began trolleying the boxes towards the fleet of lorries waiting on the shore side of the market hall . . . and everywhere the neon lights shone on the glinting, silver-grey harvest.

Cod and haddock, sole and herring, mackerel, ling, dabs and the rest. A few boxes of prawns and crab.

Here and there an occasional, dying flap of a tail or wave of a claw. Carrick had seen it countless times before but still found it compelling in its fascination and if he let his mind linger on it too long, vaguely sad. Men risked death to gather this particular harvest, which meant death in turn to the fish they netted. But once ashore the whole matter became the simple buying and selling of a raw material, top prices for the shop counters, lower for freezing, the rest for pet food or pulp processing. Business pure and simple, landsmen's business and landsmen's profit.

'Webb –' Bill Duart was back, elbowing him impatiently. Carrick came back to the present and saw the stout, middle-aged, heavily moustached figure at Duart's side. A business suit, stiff white collar, plain dark tie and the thick notebook protruding from one pocket provided their own identification.

'This is John Speke,' said Duart briskly. 'One of the wholesalers' agents here. I've told him you're interested in the *Blue Vine*.'

Speke nodded heavily and when he spoke his voice was a cautious rumble. 'Depends on what you want to know. I don't mind helping Fishery Protection, but – well, it doesn't help me if I make myself unpopular in the process.'

'You won't be involved, Mr Speke,' Carrick reassured him wryly. 'You know Jenkins Batford?'

'Well enough. He knows his trade.' From a wholesaler, it amounted to high praise. 'Mind, he can be awkward, but that goes for most of them.'

A twinkle in his eyes, Bill Duart helped him on. 'You said it's not long since he was in last, John.'

'Aye, this is the port just now – while the fish last, at any rate.' Speke grumbled briefly at the iniquity of nature which could change the pattern of catches from one month to another without any apparent justification in sense or season. 'Let's see now –' He dragged the notebook from his pocket and began flicking the pages. 'This is Wednesday and the *Blue Vine* was in about the end of last week. Here we are –' a stubby forefinger tapped the notebook – 'last Saturday morning it was. Came in with a few boxes of whites, not much of a catch.' He snorted at the memory. 'Not much of a price either, by Batford's reckoning.'

The tide of the auctioneers' progress was coming nearer, and Carrick saw the wholesaler beginning to fidget. But he wasn't finished. 'Remember him saying anything about how he stood financially?'

'Batford?' Speke shrugged. 'He talked about being on charter to that fishing festival up in the Sound of Jura.'

'Nothing else?' probed Carrick. 'He – well, he didn't hint at striking it lucky in any way?'

'No – and he's the type who'd keep that sort of thing to himself.' Speke's interest was roused. 'What's this about, Chief Officer? If there's anything my firm should know –'

'There isn't,' said Carrick deliberately, watching the man. 'Unless he gave you a letter to post.'

'Me?' The wholesaler shook his head, openly puzzled. Then he glanced round and his mouth hardened. The bidding was now only two rows away, the offers climbing for a batch of prime sole. 'Look, it's time I was getting back. I've some buying to do.'

'One last thing,' agreed Carrick. 'If Batford wanted someone to do him a favour, someone on shore here, who would he ask?'

Speke tucked the notebook in his pocket and gave a long sigh. 'Let's see. Probably – yes, he's fairly friendly with one of the lorry drivers, a man named Hamilton.'

Bill Duart scratched his nose with the tip of his hook and nodded. 'Joe Hamilton – I know him. Thanks, John.'

The wholesaler grunted a brief farewell and headed off in the direction of the buying. Bill Duart turned to Carrick, an unspoken question in his eyes.

'Hamilton,' nodded Carrick. 'Can we get him?'

'Yes, but not here, Webb.' Duart grinned. 'Like John Speke, he's got a reputation to maintain. Make it the mission canteen across the road. It's still quiet – I'll bring him over.'

The mission – full title, the Ayr branch of the Royal National Mission to Deep Sea Fishermen – lay a stone's throw from the market. A bright, modern, two-storey building topped by an iron railed balcony, it had a canteen and a billiard room on its ground floor. A couple of young fishermen, their heavy white seaboots folded down to mid-calf, were setting up a new frame of snooker at one of the billiard tables but the canteen was empty apart from the woman behind the counter. Carrick bought a cup of tea, carried it over to a corner table where he could watch the market from a window, and waited.

The tea had gone cold, with a greasy milk-skin on its surface, before Bill Duart strode into sight. The man at his side had a half-smoked cigarette dangling from his mouth, wore overalls, and had a vaguely apprehensive expression on his middle-aged face. They entered the mission, stopped at the canteen counter while Duart bought two cups of tea, then came over to join Carrick.

'Joe Hamilton,' introduced Duart briefly. 'Sit down, Joe – I've told you who he is.'

'Aye.' Hamilton pursed his lips, the cigarette still clamped between them. 'You fellas are usually in uniform, aren't you?'

'That's right.' Carrick flipped open one side of the borrowed raincoat for a moment then fastened it down again. 'Satisfied? Or do you want to see my warrant?'

'Nope, that'll do.' The lorryman lowered himself into the chair opposite and slowly stubbed his cigarette on his saucer. 'Well?'

'Joe feels he wouldn't like to land a friend in a jam,' explained Duart cheerfully. 'I've told him if he doesn't give us some answers he could be up to his own neck in trouble.'

'Which is just about how it stands,' agreed Carrick, inspecting the lorryman with deliberately obvious care. 'You saw Jenkins Batford when he was in here on Saturday?'

'Aye, but –'

'No "buts", Joe.' Carrick cut him short in brutal fashion without raising his voice. 'Jenkins is in trouble, you could be in trouble – and the trouble doubles every time I get a wrong answer. Understand?'

His face paling a little, Hamilton nodded.

'Good,' nodded Carrick. 'All right, Joe, did Jenkins ask you to do something for him?' He saw the sudden twitch of the lorryman's mouth and knew they'd found their man. 'A letter, Joe – a letter which wasn't to be posted right away, or in town?'

'It was – it was just a wee bit o' a favour.' Joe Hamilton gnawed anxiously on his lower lip, eyeing them both. 'Jenkins is a pal o' mine –'

'We know that,' snapped Duart, taking his cue from Carrick. 'When and where were you to do it, Joe?'

'On my Tuesday run to Glasgow.' Hamilton fumbled for his cigarettes and lit one nervously while they waited. 'I was to use the mailing box at the head post office in George Square, an' get it off before noon.'

'Remember the person it was addressed to, Joe? Somebody easy enough to remember, wasn't he?'

'Aye,' agreed the man, capitulating. 'You've got it right – one o' the Navy top brass. But look, no use askin' me what it was about. I asked Jenkins, an' he told me it was his business, private like.'

It seemed the truth and it was enough. Carrick leaned back and decided to try another tack while he had the chance. 'Know another boat called the *Anna B.*, Joe?'

'Aye, that's Skinner Jones an' his bunch.' The lorryman sniffed at the name. 'They're no friends o' mine, Jenkins says —'

'Never mind Jenkins. Seen them in harbour recently?'

Hamilton took a long gulp of tea and brightened a little at the change of subject. 'The *Anna B.* was in about a week ago wi' a few cran o' herring. Then they made a hell o' a fuss about loadin' some crates that were waiting for them.'

'Bill?' Carrick glanced at Duart but the harbourmaster shook his head. He turned back to Hamilton. 'What kind of crates?'

'Don't know – wasn't my business.' The lorryman shrugged his disinterest. 'Engine spares or the like. Only reason I remember is because one o' the boxes was heavier than the rest an' Skinner had to get help to move it to the quayside.'

The man couldn't help further. He listened warily while Carrick warned of the wrath that would fall on him if he made any attempt to pass a message to either boat then, the moment that was finished, he made a hasty and thankful escape.

'Well, you've got what you came for, Webb,' murmured Duart thoughtfully. He rubbed his hand across his chin. 'I'd say you struck oil with both of them. Jenkins Batford has that torpedo tucked away in a nice, quiet place while he puts pressure on the Navy. But what's this other business about the *Anna B.* – are they involved in it too?'

'The torpedo affair?' Carrick shook his head emphatically. 'No, I don't think so. There's something else going on out there, another reason altogether why Nathan Broom got the chop. But what it is . . .' His lips tightened as he accepted the fact that there, at any rate, he was no further forward. 'Bill, can you find out about those crates?'

'Given time,' agreed Duart. 'But right now we'd better start getting you back to that whirlybird.' He looked at his cup then poked it aside, a faint grin on his face. 'Leave now, and we could stop at a place I know on the way. Then maybe we could have a quick sample at something stronger than this stuff, eh?'

Neither could think of a single objection.

It was close on six p.m. and the last of Bill Duart's 'quick sample' was still making its presence comfortably warm within Carrick as the Wasp helicopter broke through a patch of low cloud and gave him his second chance to view Loch Rachan from the air.

The broad blue-green finger of water below was flecked with white, telling of a moderate swell penetrating from the open Sound, and without direct sunlight to brighten it the place seemed somehow cold, almost brooding. But the angling fleet was back and apparently intact, moored like a fringe around Borland jetty. *Marlin* was still at her position further out and, as the Wasp sank lower, he could see an early evening haze of smoke rising from the village chimneys.

The Wasp landed on the same field behind the police station and, once Carrick was clear, churned skywards again. He gave a last wave in its direction then started walking, heading for the shore and the Dairg Tower.

Jean MacDonald was, as usual, at the reception desk when he entered. The hotel foyer was busy with returned competitors, a hearty, noisy bunch whose rods and baskets were propped around the walls. The girl was dealing with one angler, who had some long, involved complaint about his room. Carrick hung back until the man left then crossed over quickly before anyone else seized the opportunity.

'Hello, Jean.'

'Good evening, Mr Carrick.' She smiled a welcome. 'At least you're not going to start telling me about how the fish were biting, are you?'

He grinned and shook his head. 'No, I'm looking for Alva.'

'I had that idea, and there's a wee note here for you.' She eyed him with a quizzical, half-amused interest which made him wonder just how much had passed between the two, then brought her handbag out from behind the desk and fished into its contents. 'Here we are –' she handed over a small, crumpled envelope – 'Alva said I was to keep it till you arrived, otherwise I'd have asked your Mr Bell to deliver it. He's through in the snuggery bar.'

'Again?' Carrick grinned. Clapper Bell seemed to be showing his usual genius for organizing reasons why he should be ashore. Conscious that the dark-haired girl was watching, he tore open the envelope and unfolded the single sheet it contained. Alva Leslie's handwriting was small, almost copperplate neat, but the message made him frown.

Webb,
The car Abbott hired was out for five hours yet only registered eleven miles. No real luck with the other thing, though Jean says P. Mack has seen Skinner Jones a few times. Now I want to find out why *Starglow* had to be refuelled this afternoon –

130

her tanks were near enough to full yesterday. See you. A.

P.S. I've fixed for the *Blue Vine*.

'Anything wrong, Mr Carrick?' queried the receptionist.

'No.' Nothing, except that he'd specifically told a certain redhead to keep out of trouble, advice which was obviously being ignored. He took a deep breath. 'When did she give you this, Jean?'

'A couple of hours ago. She – well, she said she'd be back by five-thirty, that the note was just in case she missed you.' The girl glanced at the clock on the wall, its hands now moving towards six-thirty, and the last of the light-heartedness vanished from her voice. 'Look, I don't know all that's happening, but if I can help –'

He shook his head and forced an encouraging smile. 'It's early enough yet, Jean. Just stay quiet about it. But when she does come in don't let her leave till I get back.'

Jean MacDonald's mouth was starting to shape another question, but he left her and went through to the snuggery bar. Clapper Bell was at a table in one corner, a half-empty – the bo'sun never rated things as half-full – mug of beer in front of him. He brightened as he saw Carrick crossing the crowded room towards him, but the look died as he sensed an air of trouble.

'Been ashore long, Clapper?'

'Half an hour, maybe.' Bell shifted a trifle uneasily. 'There was mail the Old Man wanted sent off, an' –'

'Forget that side.' Carrick's hands were widespread on the table as he leaned over. 'Clapper, have you seen the Leslie girl?'

'The wee redhead?' Bell's eyebrows rose a few millimetres. 'No, sir. What's up?'

131

'She could be stirring up more than she can handle.' Carrick sucked lightly on his teeth. 'Clapper, stay around for a spell. If she turns up, keep an eye on her.'

The Glasgow-Irishman gave a slow nod of understanding. One large fist reached out for his beer mug, he drained its contents at a steady gulp then wiped a sleeve across his mouth as he rose to his feet.

'I'll be aroun',' he promised.

Marlin's duty launch was at the jetty when he arrived. The coxswain nodded to the bowman the moment Carrick's feet touched the deck, they cast off, and the launch headed out, threading its way through the moored boats while the seaman's hands spun the little steering wheel with a cheerful ease.

'How'd you like the helicopter trip, sir?'

'Better than walking,' said Carrick absently, his eyes fixed on the craft they passed. *Blue Vine* and the *Anna B.* were both there, cooking smoke curling lazily from their galley stacks. But *Starglow* was out.

The coxswain started to say something else then changed his mind, shrugged a little, and thought instead, of what he'd do when he came off watch. If the first mate was in a private lather it wasn't his affair – he'd enough troubles of his own.

Once alongside the fishery cruiser, Carrick wasted no time in getting aboard. As he reached the top of the companion ladder, a familiar growl greeted him and Captain Shannon stepped forward from the shadow of the bridge.

'Right, mister.' Shannon beckoned with a crooked finger, led the way through the nearest door into the oily, gently throbbing warmth of the ship, and straight on until they reached his day cabin. He gestured Carrick to go in, followed, then let the door swing shut. 'Well?'

132

'Jenkins Batford, sir. We located the man who mailed the letter for him.'

'Aye.' Shannon gave a long sigh of acceptance. 'Well, so it was genuine. I'm almost sorry.'

'Sir?' Carrick looked at him blankly.

Shannon's mouth twisted a little, as if tasting an unpleasant morsel. 'The village constable had a telephone call this afternoon – anonymous variety. According to the man at the other end we should keep an eye on the *Blue Vine* tonight if we wanted to "find something to our advantage".' He growled into his beard, his eyes diamond hard. 'Well, it fits. With this oil rig coming through the Navy will be out of the exercise area and our angling friends aren't likely to be around. We'll be on sailing readiness from an hour before dusk. If Batford takes the drifter out we shadow her – Pettigrew ran another full check on our radar and whatever was wrong is cured. When Batford stops we give him a little time then go in and clean up this whole blasted mess.'

'If it is the whole mess, sir.' Carrick said it quietly, and saw Shannon's face change into a scowl. 'What about the other boat in the Sound last night? And there's more –'

'More?' The scowl deepened. 'Mister, I've already enough, boats or no boats. I've had Department checking files. Years back, when Batford wasn't much older than you are, his family had a stand-up compensation row with the Admiralty. They had a boat sunk in collision with a fleet auxiliary, lost the case, and just about all they owned with it. From his standpoint he's got motive.'

'For murder?' Carrick met Shannon's withering glare and waited deliberately until it died a little. 'Maybe that's just what someone is hoping we'll believe. But suppose it's totally separate.'

For a moment the fiery little Superintendent of Fisheries stood silent, his mouth clamped shut. Then, at last, he nodded with a grim authority. 'Have your say, Mister Carrick. You've a certain right to it, but it had better be good.'

'Let's begin right back with something we know, that Nathan Broom wasn't killed for any casual reason,' said Carrick grimly. 'Then add up all the bits and pieces we've got that don't make sense –'

Shannon heard him out, once or twice apparently on the brink of interrupting but each time restraining himself to a nod of acknowledgement. When Carrick had finished, the small, bearded figure rocked slowly back and forward for a spell then, still saying nothing, walked over to the cabin porthole and looked out. At last, he turned.

'If the girl's right, there's one reason why Abbott's launch needed refuelling,' his voice grated. 'They could have transferred what they had in their tanks to refuel the other boat we're looking for, mister. But what was in those cases Skinner Jones loaded at Ayr, eh?'

'Bill Duart's trying to find out,' said Carrick. He felt a sense of relief, the knowledge that, as far as Shannon's views were concerned, he'd won.

'And the girl?' queried Shannon, a suddenly worried note in his voice. 'Where is she now?'

'I don't know,' confessed Carrick. 'I left Clapper Bell ashore and told him to keep his eyes open.'

'Hmmph.' Shannon paced the cabin, stopped, and in sheer habit tapped the barometer glass on the wall. 'Rising a little.' He snorted briefly. 'Well, isn't it about time you tried to find out? But don't expect any help from Superintendent Neilson or that sergeant of his. They've gone off to Campbeltown on some idea or other.'

The launch took Carrick back to the jetty, and once again he headed for the Dairg Tower. Hands in his pockets, a cigarette in his mouth, Clapper Bell was leaning rather sadly against the hotel doorway. As he saw Carrick approach he straightened a little and shook his head.

'No sign o' her yet, sir. But I got the address where she's stayin' from that girl Jean. Maybe we could try there, eh?'

They set off together. The place was a white, slate-roofed cottage on the upper fringe of the village. Fronted by a small garden, it had lace curtains in the windows and the door knocker was a piece of worn, polished brass. Carrick rapped twice, they waited, and eventually the door clicked and swung open a few inches.

'Well?' The woman who looked out was thin and elderly with short, grey hair and ramrod-straight shoulders. She wore a black dress of some shiny material as if it was a natural outer shell, and her lips were already pursed disapprovingly. 'What do you want here?'

'We're looking for Miss Leslie –' began Carrick.

'Then you've a disappointment due,' sniffed the woman. 'She's out, and never bothered to say when she'd be back. Anyway, my paying guests aren't allowed callers.' She inspected them acidly. 'Particularly of the opposite sex and especially sea-going individuals.'

The door slammed shut.

'Who's the old biddy callin' a "sea-goin' individual"?' growled Clapper Bell indignantly. 'Hell, you wouldn't catch me dossin' in there, that's for sure.'

Carrick nudged him on. In the next quarter hour they covered most of the village, asked at the garage, the general store, even looked in at the police cottage. At the finish, they'd still drawn a blank and Carrick's concern was growing by the minute. The return trip to the Dairg Tower led past the jetty and he slowed, a thoughtful expression on his face. The *Anna B.* had been moved in and was lying alongside the piers with the hatch boards removed from her fish hold but no sign of life on her deck.

'No sense in lookin' there,' said Bell flatly. 'She's been lyin' out in the loch all afternoon.' He glanced at Carrick. 'Well, I'd say the girl's gone an' landed herself in some kind o' a jam. What's next on the programme?'

'The hotel again,' decided Carrick grimly. 'I'll check with Jean MacDonald. If there's nothing new, then it's time I had another talk with Shannon.'

The Dairg Tower's foyer was quieter this time, with most of the guests gone to dinner. As Carrick entered, Jean MacDonald glanced at him from the reception desk and slowly shook her head. While Clapper Bell mumbled about a need for cigarettes and headed towards the snuggery he started over to the girl.

'Looking for me, Chief Officer?' Peter Mack was halfway down the stairway and descended the rest in exuberant style, their previous brushes apparently forgotten. 'You've heard the news?'

'About what?' Carrick regarded him woodenly. The hotelier stood in front of him, rubbing his hands and apparently pleased with the world in general.

'Today's festival – over two and a half tons catch in total. No records broken, but an excellent start.' He gave a sly smile. 'Might even have been better if you hadn't had to chase some of our naughtier entrants, eh?'

'They did well enough from what I saw,' said Carrick with little interest. 'What happens to the fish?'

'Marketed, sold, and proceeds after expenses to charity,' declared Mack with an unctuous self-approval. 'Now, can I help you?'

Carrick nodded towards the snuggery. 'Just waiting on our bo'sun.'

'Petty Officer Bell?' Mack chuckled. 'Yes, I've seen him a few times.' He came closer, his voice more confidential. 'I was wondering if you'd arranged to meet Miss Leslie.'

'No.' Carrick kept his voice neutral, his face expressionless. 'Why?'

The hotelier shrugged. 'Two reasons, really. If you had, you could tell her I've arranged with Jenkins Batford that she can go out with the *Blue Vine* tomorrow. And, if you're not, I was hoping you and Captain Shannon might find time to come ashore to – well, a little private party late this evening.' He moistened his lips a little. 'We – ah – have had one or two disagreements, I know. But I'd like to establish what you might call a better understanding.'

'Sorry.' Carrick shook his head. 'I don't think we'll be available.'

'You mean you're going out?' Mack raised an eyebrow. 'There's no contest session tonight.'

'We're still on stand-by call,' said Carrick vaguely, and was glad to see Clapper Bell coming back towards them. 'Maybe some other time.'

Mack escorted them to the door. Outside, as it closed again, Bell shook his head. 'That's a creep if I ever saw one. Any word o' the girl, sir?'

'Nothing.'

'Pity.' The Glasgow-Irishman was gruffly sympathetic. 'You know, I saw somethin' strange in the bar back there. The *Blue Vine* boys aren't supposed to have any love for the *Anna B.* bunch, right?'

'That's how it's reckoned,' agreed Carrick.

'Aye.' Bell flipped open his new pack of cigarettes, offered one to Carrick, took another for himself, and struck a match to light both. 'Well, when I went in there's Skinner Jones at a corner table wi' the lad who's engineer on *Blue Vine*. Fellow who usually wears a leather jacket, Davey –'

'Davey Gwynne. Long dark hair and not much to say for himself.'

'That's him,' agreed Bell. 'Well, whatever was goin' on, Skinner Jones was doin' the talkin' and Gwynne didn't seem to like what he was hearing.' As usual he'd saved the choicest item till last. 'First time I've seen Gwynne without that jacket, an' with shirt sleeves rolled up. He's ex-Navy like mysel'.' He stopped, and pulled up his own jacket and shirt cuff, exposing a hairy forearm, liberally tattooed. 'See this anchor? I had it done in Hong Kong when I was made up to leadin' rating. Gwynne's got one that's different – a leadin' torpedoman's badge.'

'It figures,' said Carrick mildly.

'Aye, that's what I thought.' *Marlin*'s bo'sun was disappointed at the limited effect of his news. He drew hard on his cigarette. 'Want me to stay around?'

Carrick nodded. He was tired of waiting and hoping. It was time to do something positive.

Captain Shannon was just finishing the ritual of his evening constitutional, five times clockwise, five times anti-clockwise round *Marlin*'s boat deck when Carrick came aboard. He stopped, hands clasped behind his back, heard his Chief Officer's report in a frowning silence, then grunted.

'Let's walk a spell, mister.' As Carrick fell obediently into step the older man paced slowly and deliberately along. As they passed the wireless cabin, the crackle of static reached their ears from a half-opened porthole. Shannon nodded in its direction. 'Had a signal while you were gone, from Duart at Ayr. The crates for the *Anna B.* were delivered by truck, listed as engine spares – no consignee's name on the labels.'

138

They'd done another half-turn of the deck before he spoke again. 'Well, out with it. There's something on your mind.'

Carrick halted by the rail, leaned against it, and nodded. 'I'd like to take a look at Garra Island, sir. That's where we found *Starglow* this morning, with Abbott making a fuss about fishing a place no one else would dream of trying.'

'It's no crime.' Shannon rubbed his beard, looking past him out across the loch. 'I know how you feel about the girl, man. But I've asked around the ship while you were gone. We've two of our own men who saw *Starglow* leave the loch at about three this afternoon – by your own account that's almost an hour before Alva Leslie disappeared.'

'Can they say who was aboard?' countered Carrick.

'No.' *Marlin*'s captain showed his dislike of the situation. 'Even so, privately I might like to do something about it. But that's impossible. *Marlin*'s job, and mine, is to stay here until the *Blue Vine* goes out.'

'If I had Clapper Bell, the scuba gear and the packboat –'

'If. And if you went down to Garra and if –' Shannon put a heavy emphasis on the word again – 'if there was anyone there you'd be spotted miles away. They'd be watching, bound to be.' One foot tapped the deck in thoughtful fashion. 'What's the time?'

Carrick glanced at his watch. 'Coming up for seven forty-five, sir.'

'Let's be formal and say near enough to twenty hundred hours,' mused Shannon. 'All right, I'm not expecting the *Blue Vine* to move till nightfall. Wait till twenty-two hundred, mister. If there's no sign of the girl by then you can have Bell and the packboat. That way, it should be near enough dusk when you're off

Garra. But remember, you'll be on your own from there on, whatever happens.'

Carrick knew better than to thank him. 'I'll settle for that. What about Superintendent Neilson?'

'He's still at Campbeltown, but we can get some kind of message to him if she doesn't show up. Anyway, if this home-knitted theory of yours is even halfway right the less fuss we make about things the better it could be for that girl.' He gave a sudden growl, strode over to the aft searchlight platform, rubbed one finger over the paintwork, and inspected the result in disgust. 'Filthy . . . once this is finished I'm going to have all hands clean this ship until it's a little less like a floating pigsty. Understood, mister?'

Solemnly, Carrick nodded.

After an hour, Shannon sent two men ashore to relieve Clapper Bell. At nine-forty, still no word from the shore, the packboat was quietly lowered from *Marlin*'s stern and the two sets of scuba gear loaded aboard.

Ten o'clock came. On the bridge, Shannon watched through binoculars as one of the deckhands posted ashore walked casually along to the end of the jetty, stopped to light a cigarette then waved a hand casually across his chest as if to extinguish the match.

'That's it.' Shannon laid aside the binoculars and glanced at Carrick, waiting at his side. 'Well, right or wrong, mister – good luck.' As Carrick turned to go, the little Superintendent of Fisheries cleared his throat. 'Webb –'

'Sir?'

A trifle embarrassed, Shannon clawed briefly at his beard. 'Watch it – you know what I mean. It takes a long time to break in new deck officers.'

Carrick grinned, and an answering twinkle lit in Shannon's eyes.

Three minutes later, the wind light from the south-west, the sea gently calm, the packboat purred quietly away from the fishery cruiser's stern. The sky was dulling, with fresh, gathering cloud, and the sun had gone down below the horizon.

Clapper Bell was at the outboard's helm, whistling softly as the little rubber-hulled craft headed for the open Sound. Carrick settled himself into a more comfortable position beside the scuba gear and watched the water ripple past, then begin to foam as the throttle gradually opened.

Right or wrong, Shannon had said. Well, they'd soon find out.

Chapter Seven

Roughly an hour after clearing Loch Rachan the grey shape of Garra Island loomed ahead in the gathering dusk. As it grew nearer, Clapper Bell gradually eased the packboat's engine back to a whisper – sound carried far on a quiet sea – while Carrick blessed the fact that their tiny craft could be little more than a speck on the water.

They took turn about, one at the helm, the other changing into his scuba suit, then cut the outboard altogether with still roughly a mile remaining. Bell unshipped the stub-handled paddles from the emergency kit and, crouched low, soon sweating within the rubber folds of the scuba suits, they worked their way on. Carrick's target was a cluster of rocks rising from the water about five hundred yards to the northwest of the main bulk of the island, his one fear that they might yet be seen. But their luck appeared in, the packboat reached the cluster's shelter, and they let the light swell bring the packboat in until it bumped gently against the dark, raw granite.

The grapnel out, the boat secured, they wriggled into the aqualung harnesses.

'Remember the drill, Clapper,' said Carrick softly. 'Stay together, no fuss unless it's necessary.'

'Aye.' There was a tinge of doubt in the bo'sun's voice. 'Mind, I still think we'd do the job a mite quicker if we took a side each.'

'And if something happened on the way?' Carrick shook his head. His flippers were comfortably firm and the cork-handled, double-edged diving knife, one edge heavily serrated, was secure in its leg-sheath. 'Let's go.'

They eased over the side into the chill, chest-high water, worked their way out to clear the rest of the rocks, then duck-dived down. Dark shadows side by side beneath the surface, they began finning, legs moving in a smooth, regular crawl-beat. Tendrils of weed brushed against them briefly, then the bottom shelved away. Demand regulator valve clicking steadily, a thin trail of exhaled air bubbling from his outlet tube, Carrick counted a full five minutes before he gestured upwards and they rose to the surface.

As the water cleared from the face-mask glass he had his first close-up view of Garra. The initial blur shaped into a peaceful, empty scene of pebbled beach, rock, and the low, salt-stunted grass beyond. They were about a hundred yards out, the rest of Garra's two-thirds of a mile circumference lay waiting. He glanced round at Clapper Bell, raised finger and thumb together in a brief signal, and sank down again.

They repeated the process every few hundred yards, moving gradually round the island's shore. Once, their heads bobbing up out of the water, the face-masks like single, monstrous eyes, sent a family of grey seals panicking off a nearby shelf of rock where they'd been resting. Further on, Clapper Bell had to use his knife as he became briefly entangled in a swath of undersea vegetation.

At the southern limit of the beach they'd still drawn a blank. Starting up the eastern shore, where the bottom was more inclined to sand and sediment, Carrick fought a growing tension. Right or wrong . . . the first time they surfaced there was nothing but the inevitable empty shore. The second time was the same. The third, he looked around as his vision cleared, saw an apparent emptiness, and sensed Clapper Bell bobbing at his side, ready to go down again.

But the place seemed familiar. He floated for a moment, saw the small headland to the north, and recognized the place as close to the spot where he'd found Abbott's *Starglow* fishing that morning. The water swirled, and Clapper Bell bumped against him.

The Glasgow-Irishman removed the breathing tube from his mouth, spat out some sea-water he'd come close to swallowing, grinned, and pointed.

'Over there, sir – see it?' he said softly.

Carrick hadn't till then – and there was reason.

To their right, a low rock face displaced the shingle beach. Hard under its dark grey shadow, merging into the only slighter grey of the fast failing light, a draping of heavy camouflage netting hung like a veil over two boats. The one nearest the shore was *Starglow*, its slim, cream hull almost completely obscured. The other, tied alongside, was an old motor fisher – maybe thirty feet long, painted a dull black, foremast lowered and deckhouse reduced to little more than a waist-high shelter.

They sank down, swam closer, and surfaced cautiously. The motor fisher had no name on her bow, and, like the cabin launch, had no sign of life on her deck. But, as he floated, Carrick saw *Starglow*'s cockpit door swing open. Behind the camouflage nets one vague figure then another emerged, crossed to the motor fisher, and vanished again somewhere near her bow. They reappeared a moment later, crossed back to the cabin launch and when he saw them next they were ashore, clearly visible – Page Abbott and the burly Douglas Swanson.

144

The two figures stopped, there was the quick flare of a match, the pinprick glow of a cigarette in the gloom, then the men moved on, disappearing behind a jutting shoulder of rock.

Carrick tapped Clapper Bell on the shoulder, signalled again, and they flippered gently towards the two boats. They reached the shelter of the motor fisher's hull, steadied themselves against its side, then looked at each other with a bewildered surprise. The fisher was sheathed from deck to waterline in a dark, sticky, foam-like material. Carrick drew a hand along it and traces of the substance stuck to his fingers like some tenacious slime.

'What the hell kind o' stuff's that?' asked the bo'sun in a hoarse whisper.

'No idea.' Carrick shook his head. 'But we'll check *Starglow*, then go in down-beach.'

Starglow's hull was untreated. Carrick restrained an impulse to board her, shoved away from the cabin launch's side, and minutes later they landed behind broken rock about two hundred yards to the south, left the aqualungs hidden at the base of one large chunk of granite, and were ready.

The moon was starting to come up, a pale glow in the still dull-lit summer sky, as they left the beach and started to crawl inland across the rough, spear-stubbled grass. They travelled in a curve, aiming for an area above and a little way beyond the spot where they'd last seen Abbott and Swanson.

'On ahead,' murmured Clapper Bell, gesturing him down. They lay and listened, heard the sound of metal on metal, then the murmur of voices, and slowly edged forward.

When they stopped, they were on the lip of a small hollow. On the far side was the jutting shoulder of rock and beyond that again the sea. Down in the shelter of the hollow the two men were working at a strange framework of slim, tubular steel topped by what looked, at first, like a metal shield. Other equipment lay around, and Carrick's fingernails bit into the palms of his hands as Abbott crossed over, returning carrying a small, obviously heavy box, and handed it over to Swanson with deliberate care. It all made sense now – shattering, almost unbelievable sense.

'Back, Clapper –' there was a strange, almost strangled note in his voice.

'Eh?' The bo'sun wriggled round on his side. 'Something –' he saw Carrick's broad-boned face, grim and still, and obeyed without another word.

Carrick led him back in another crawl to the rocks where they'd left the aqualungs, squatted on his haunches once they were in cover, and stayed silent for a moment. When he did speak, the very lack of emotion in his manner was as telling as his earlier reaction. 'Clapper, remember when *Marlin* came up to Loch Rachan to start this job?'

'The night run?' Clapper Bell nodded. That was still less than forty-eight hours back, though even to him it was beginning to seem an age away. 'What about it, sir?'

'After we arrived, the Old Man complained about the radar readings. Something had gone wrong for a spell. Were you there when it happened?'

The bo'sun scratched his bristling head. 'Aye, he got a fuzzy pickup, what looked like a double image.'

Carrick drew a deep breath. 'Where?'

'The Camas Dubh channel,' said Bell without hesitation. 'It happened when the screen was registerin' one o' these blacklight beacons –' He stopped, his mouth hanging open.

'The deep-water racon,' nodded Carrick. 'That's what they've got down there, Clapper. A lightweight version, able to give a duplicate signal – and if they're using it tonight, then they're out to catch something really big.'

His companion blinked. 'Is there anythin' on the move?'

For once, it seemed, Clapper Bell's grapevine contacts had let him down. Slowly, Carrick nodded. 'The *Sea Raven*, a new floating oil rig. Call her two million pounds of somebody's money – and she needs the deep channel.'

Clapper Bell swore once in surprise then a second time with a bitter understanding.

The racon beacons, floating buoys with a reflector-like disc at their peaks, had been nicknamed 'black-lights' by the West Coast fishermen almost from the day they made their first appearance. And it was apt . . . provided the person hearing the nickname had even a basic understanding of radar.

A ship's radar received an image on its screen which was really a record of signal waves it sent out being bounced back from objects ahead. This was fine when it came to registering other ships or a firm coast-line, but it left the problem of navigating channels where low, sandy shores gave a fuzzy, indistinct image or where hidden shoal rock lay waiting.

There were lighthouses, like the Whip Rock. There were light buoys. But the modern answer, impervious to fog and similar hazards, was the transponder, the racon marker. When the probing beam from a ship's radar met its reflector the invisible impact stirred the beacon's electronic heart to life – and it answered with a coded response.

How Page Abbott meant to do it, Carrick could only guess. But that substitute blacklight being prepared in the hollow made sense out of the little piece of paper he'd found, the paper with the two triangles.

Three blacklight markers acted as guides for the main deep-water channel through the Camas Dubh

147

channel. They made no difference to normal coastal traffic, which steered a straight course on a bearing from the Whip Light. But any deep-draught vessel's navigation depended on holding a line from the lighthouse until she had the first marker on her port side, then steering a tight course which kept the next two to starboard. Move just one marker, throw out the triangulation, and the ship concerned would gut its underbelly on hidden fangs of rock.

'This *Sea Raven*, sir –' Clapper Bell gnawed his lower lip – 'any idea when she's comin' through?'

'Tonight sometime, that's all I know.' Carrick glanced at his watch, the luminous dial bright and clear. 'Clapper, get back to the packboat, take it –' He stopped, thinking for a moment. They were about twelve miles from Loch Rachan, a few less to the north of Whip Light. The mainland shore lay nearer than either choice, but the odds were against finding a telephone on that desolate coastline. 'Look, try for Whip Light. Jumbo Wills is there, and they've got radio.'

'Makes sense,' agreed Bell softly. 'Wi' the tide startin' on the ebb I'll gain a bit o' extra pace from the current.' He frowned. 'What about you?'

'There's Alva – and that beacon.'

'Aye.' The word carried a considerable understanding. 'That's what I thought.' Bell turned to reach for his aqualung harness.

A few yards away, a pebble rattled. A second later a powerful torch-beam cut through the gloom, pinning them in its light.

'Stay just like that, both of you,' said a woman's cool, acid voice.

'Better do what Marge says,' advised Page Abbott, a shape moving a little to the left of the torch. 'There's a shotgun on you, Carrick. Twenty gauge, buckshot loaded – at this range even Swanson couldn't miss. Hands on your head, please.'

To reinforce the advice they heard the low double click of the hammers being cocked. Carrick stood very still for a moment then glanced at Clapper Bell and nodded. Slowly, they obeyed.

'Fine.' *Starglow*'s owner crunched over the shingle towards them, an automatic pistol in his right hand. Swanson and Marge Harding followed, Swanson with the shotgun's butt pressed tight under one elbow, the twin muzzles pointed squarely in their direction. Abbott reached them first and, carefully avoiding coming between them and the shotgun, inspected his captives.

'We'll have these.' He stopped, collected the two diving knives, and tossed them carelessly beside the aqualungs. 'That's better.'

'Maybe there's more of them around,' suggested Swanson with a nervous caution.

'No.' Marge Harding was positive. 'I told you, just the two.'

'You were unlucky, Carrick,' explained Abbott smoothly. 'We left Marge doing her sentry act on the headland. She was on her way back to say it was getting too dark to be worthwhile hanging on when she spotted you crawling around up there.'

'Want us to congratulate her?' asked Clapper Bell bitterly.

'Hardly.' Abbott's pale face twitched a little at the idea then he became suddenly business-like. 'The hands stay as they are for the moment. Head for *Starglow*, Carrick – and be sensible about it.'

They set off in procession along the beach, across the rocks beyond, and finally over the narrow plank-walk on to the cabin launch's deck. Abbott approached the business of going below with razor-edged care. He opened the cockpit door, stopped to switch on the lights in the below-deck cabin, then went down the companionway ladder. At the bottom, he stopped and ordered them to follow.

The shotgun above, the pistol below, Carrick and Clapper Bell shuffled down. As Marge Harding and Swanson followed, Carrick looked around. The two men were in dark slacks and heavy, dark sweaters. Marge Harding wore a dark green one-piece suit, cut in battledress lines and elasticized at wrist and ankles. Around the cabin, the porthole deadlights were already closed to guard against any tell-tale glimmer to the outside world. The black leather settees along each side were littered with trimmed fragments of electrical cable.

'You've been busy,' he said grimly.

'We have.' Abbott passed the pistol, a .380 Browning, to Marge Harding as he spoke. She took it clumsily, but there was no change in her face, her finger was on the trigger, and it stayed pointed firmly in their direction. 'Now, we'll just organize things a little better.'

The man crossed to one of the bulkhead lockers, took out a bobbin reel of nylon line, brought a pen-knife from his pocket, and made a swift, scientific job of tying their hands together behind their backs. As an added refinement, he made a separate job of lashing their thumbs.

Carrick winced as the nylon cut into his flesh. 'Being thorough, aren't you?'

'It pays.' Abbott tightened the last knot and stood back. 'Unfortunately, the fact you're here means we haven't been quite thorough enough somewhere along the way. Right, sit down – both of you.' As they did, he took the automatic again from Marge Harding and glanced at Swanson. 'Better get up top, just in case. And take that shotgun with you – it makes me nervous.'

Swanson grunted and headed for the ladder. As his feet sounded on the deck above their heads, Marge Harding, the cabin lights glinting like frost on her blue-rinsed hair, showed a mixture of anxiety and impatience.

'What do we do with them, Page?'

'Do?' Abbott gave a slightly malicious grin. 'Have a talk, I think, until our other little absent friend arrives.' He regarded Carrick narrowly. 'I mean the girl, Carrick. You came looking for her, correct?'

'Among other things.'

'Then you're too early, Mr Carrick,' said Marge Harding curtly. 'About an hour too early.' She glanced at Abbott. 'Page, from where they were they'd see –'

'The beacon?' Abbott nodded, took out his cigarettes, lit one, then thumbed over his shoulder to the little galley aft. 'Marge, I could use some coffee.' She hesitated, and he winked at her. 'They're safe enough.'

'All right.' Almost reluctantly, she went away.

The Browning dangling loose between his fingers, Page Abbott turned to face Carrick again, his manner hardening several degrees. 'So you came looking for Alva Leslie, little rubber suits and all. But why here, Carrick?'

'Too many things that didn't fit, like that hire car's mileage, and finding you here this morning, fishing a non-existent mark.'

'The mark, of course.' Abbott nodded his understanding. 'You gave us quite a fright then. And the car – that would be Miss Leslie again, I suppose. Funny thing is, we originally wanted someone like her to complete our picture of a happy angling outing. Then –'

'Then Nathan Broom stuck his nose in, and knew too much about radar?' queried Carrick. He tried to ease the nylon bands on his wrist and grimaced. 'If

151

you'd made a better job of weighing him down you might have got away with it.'

'It wasn't –' Abbott stopped and shrugged his slim shoulders. 'Let's say these things happen. And, yes, frankly Broom's – ah – disposal upset our schedule.'

'The hell with your schedule,' growled Clapper Bell. 'What about the girl?'

'On her way here now, Petty Officer,' soothed Abbott. His eyes flickered briefly, almost regretfully. 'I had a radio call advising me she'd been collected. You'll see her, both of you – just as soon as Skinner Jones gets here with the *Anna B.*'

'Then you go out after the *Sea Raven*?' Carrick's mouth tightened. 'Abbott, you may as well forget it. Even if that substitute blacklight worked –'

'So you even know about our target?' Abbott was either a master at controlling his feelings or possessed a supreme confidence – it was hard to tell which. 'Maybe I owe you a slight apology, Carrick. You've done much better than I'd imagined.' He took a last draw on the cigarette, stubbed it, and his free hand smoothed over his thin, mousey hair. 'But you've only just fitted the pieces together, correct?'

'That's your problem, pal,' growled Clapper Bell.

Abbott shook his head. 'Don't try to frighten me. If Captain Shannon or that heather-clump detective Neilson had any idea about tonight they'd be here. No, *Marlin's* main business right now is the *Blue Vine* and Jenkins Batford – and Batford will go out to collect his torpedo. I know that for sure.'

'The engineer?' Carrick knew a dull sense of despair at the raw truth behind the words.

'The young man with the tattooed arm,' nodded Abbott. 'He's loyal, but indiscreet after a few drinks, and Skinner Jones can be a convivial host.'

'Convivial rattlesnake, you mean.' Carrick's head jerked up. 'Shannon knows we're here.'

'Perhaps.' Abbott broke off as Marge Harding came from the galley carrying three mugs of coffee on a small tin tray. His voice softened a little. 'Thank you, my dear.' He took the nearest mug, sipped, and nodded his satisfaction. 'I was just explaining to our friends that I find no cause for undue alarm in their being here.'

'But I do.' The tall, slender woman looked bleakly in their direction. 'We'll need to – well, get rid of them, won't we?'

Abbott nodded an almost casual agreement. 'We can discuss the details once Skinner Jones arrives. But there won't be need to involve you.' He sipped his mug again. 'Better give one of those up to Swanson, Marge – then if you take over watch again for a spell he can complete his checks on the beacon.'

She nodded and went up the companionway, balancing the tray in one hand. Abbott watched her progress with something close to affection.

An elbow nudging his side made Carrick turn. Clapper Bell's lips mouthed silently, and he nodded towards their captor. Swiftly, Carrick shook his head. A time might come, but for now any attempt to jump the man would be an invitation to suicide. He wanted to keep Abbott talking, find out what he could, while he could.

'How are you going to work it, Abbott – sink one of the racon buoys and float your own?'

'Nothing so crude.' Abbott crossed leisurely to the settee opposite, sank down on the leather, and stretched his legs out with a relaxed sigh. 'I'm not taking all the credit. Call me more – well, a middleman, an organizer. Swanson is the expert. However fat and stupid he looks, he's well qualified in radar technology, trained at Government expense. He held down a research and development job until he was removed from it under a slight cloud – but he's kept himself up-to-date on the subject.'

'A bent boffin,' groaned Clapper Bell. 'That's all anyone ruddy well needs.'

'It's all we – ah – ruddy well needed,' corrected Abbott. 'His racon unit matches the code response from one of the Camas Dubh transponders. We've spent a lot of time making sure since we got here. We'll mount it on the *Anna B.*, she'll take up position, our position and –' he smacked the barrel of the Browning against the settee. 'That's how it'll be. The other part depends on that old tub we've got alongside. We temporarily disconnect the genuine racon unit –'

'But any radar screen will still pick up its reflector image,' reminded Carrick, puzzled by the cool confidence of the man.

'Old-fashioned thinking,' sneered Abbott. 'Weren't you taught some materials reflect an image better than others? The same holds good at the other end of the scale – some materials are poor reflectors. The Germans, very thorough people, developed a plastifoam coating towards the end of World War Two which completely absorbed a radar impulse. They had started to use it for U-boat pen camouflage, and other people have worked on it since. A really skilled radar man can still spot something wrong – but a ship's officer, navigating a channel, seeing the correct number of beacons on his screen?' He shook his head. 'He'll accept what he sees, our beacon. The other will be screened by a plastifoam curtain – the motor fisher's already coated.'

Carrick remembered the sticky, dark slime he'd encountered and nodded grimly. 'All right, but what about afterwards? There's going to be plenty of questions asked.'

154

'But where?' Abbott grinned. 'We'll sink our own gear with the motor fisher in a nice deep part of the Sound. The genuine beacon will be back in action. *Starglow* will be back in Loch Rachan long before anything happens – and if you're thinking of the *Anna B.*, she's on a scheduled run to Ayr with approximately two tons of fish, this morning's festival catch.' He grunted, tiring of the game. 'It won't all be as smooth as we wanted, Carrick. And I'll admit the *Blue Vine*'s torpedo was a gift as a diversion, that we might be in trouble without it. But we'll get there.'

'Why?' Carrick started to rise up, but the gun waved him down again. 'What do you gain from it, Abbott?'

'Money,' said the man briefly. 'A lot of it. Stock exchange style. Starting in about two hours' time if that oil rig tow is anything like on schedule.' He sat back, lit a cigarette, and showed no sign of wanting to talk further.

Chin on chest, Carrick stared down at the cabin's decking. He had more than a glimmer of an idea of what Abbott meant. The Nanda Group weren't big as oil firms went, but he knew that when the 1700 mile North Sea exploration area was parcelled out under Government licences they'd managed to get four block sites. Probably they'd scraped the bottom of their cash barrel to finance the building of their oil rig platform. A major delay for, at best, salvage and repairs, at worst, the attempted financing and building of a replacement, might see them bankrupt.

The North Sea oil and gas search had been christened the greatest financial gamble of the century. When firms went into it they knew somebody had to lose, even if there were rich dividends for the fortunate.

But they couldn't be expected to reckon on brutal, cold-blooded sabotage lengthening the odds against them. And when a firm went bust – well, Carrick knew at least enough to realize there was always someone around to pick up the pieces at a juicy profit.

He and Clapper and maybe Alva were the only people who knew enough to stop what lay ahead. Yet the tight, fine line so firm round his wrists gave little hope of that chance – little hope, either, of them still being alive by morning.

There were exactly seven minutes left before midnight when Marge Harding came down to say that the *Anna B.* was coming in. She took over guard from Abbott and, as the latter hurried up towards the cockpit, she sat down in his place. Her face was as coldly expressionless as marble, only the way her free hand stayed clenched knuckle-tight at her side told of the tension within.

Soon, they heard the slow, distinctive beat of a fishing boat engine. A minute later there were voices, then *Starglow*'s hull shuddered briefly as the new arrival bumped alongside the old motor fisher tied next to them and the impact was transmitted on. More voices and the rapid footsteps of several men were followed by the grating of loads being dragged across the cabin launch's deck. Then, at last, Page Abbott came back down the companionway ladder followed by Skinner Jones.

'There they are, all ready for collection – just like I said,' declared Abbott briskly.

'Aye.' The *Anna B.*'s skipper was in his customary jersey and overalls and seemed far from happy as he regarded the two Fishery Protection men. 'But I don't like any o' this, Mr Abbott, an' the crew won't. If there was another way –'

'Not unless you all fancy a long term in some jail,' said Abbott, turning towards him. 'Don't tell me you're having trouble with your conscience, Skinner. Not at this stage.' He waited a moment, then glanced back at Carrick. 'You'll be interested to know *Marlin* has quit Loch Rachan. She's following the *Blue Vine*, and they're heading north.'

Clapper Bell shrugged, but for once didn't reply. Ignoring the gun opposite, Carrick struggled to his feet. 'Does that really change things, Skinner?' As the drifter skipper avoided his gaze, Carrick tried again. 'You're still not in too deep. And there's the girl –'

Abbott took one step nearer, then the back of his hand smashed against Carrick's mouth, leaving an angry red weal.

'Stay quiet,' he snapped. 'Ready, Skinner?'

Skinner Jones had two spots of colour on his thin, high cheekbones. He rubbed the palms of his hands against his overalls, hesitated a moment, then shrugged. 'Let's get on with it,' he said tonelessly.

They were hustled up on deck, where a couple of low-powered lights shining from the *Anna B.*'s foremast illuminated the scene. Already the camouflage nets had been removed and the lightweight tubular scaffolding, brought from the shore, was lying on its side on the drifter's deck. Swanson and three of the *Anna B.*'s men were transferring another load of lesser equipment.

Carrick looked around, knowing there should be a fourth man somewhere, and saw him a moment later near the bow of the dark-hulled motor fisher still lashed to *Starglow*. Another small, lonely figure was by his side.

'Join her,' invited Abbott cynically. 'You've a lot to talk about, I'd imagine.'

The work around them slowed and curious eyes

watched as the two Fishery men were pushed across and made their stumbling way for'rard. As they reached the girl, Abbott's voice rang out.

'Let's keep on with it, lads. We haven't much of a time margin . . .' He was already heading away.

The pace quickened again. Carrick ignored it, ignored too, the sullen-faced guard at Alva Leslie's side. Hands tied behind her, clothes rumpled, the long, flame-red hair a tousled mop, she looked at him in the dull light with a mixture of shock and despair. Then, somehow, she forced a smile.

'Hello, Webb. I'd been hoping you might turn up, but –'

'But not like this?' he grimaced. 'You're all right?'

She nodded, her nose wrinkling in an attempt at humour. 'Apart from feeling I smell like a fish market – they had me stuck in the hold with the rest of the cargo.'

'How'd they get you, lass?' asked Clapper Bell gruffly, glaring at their guard with a fierce and total contempt.

'I tried to be too clever,' she confessed wryly, shivering a little in the night air. 'I left that note for Webb and left the hotel. Next thing, I was walking through a lane when – well, I was thumped on the head from behind. After that, I was in a room somewhere with a gag in my mouth and a sack over my head. All I know is it was small and empty, with stone walls. Somebody came in a couple of times, but he didn't talk.' Her mouth tightened at the memory. 'The worst bit was being shoved in a box of some kind before they loaded me on the *Anna B.*'

'Brave boys, every one,' snorted *Marlin*'s bo'sun. Their guard grinned uneasily and sidled a few paces away. Carrick sighed and rested back on the edge of the boat's side.

158

'You'd better know what we've landed in, Alva.' While the bustle of preparation continued around, he spoke quietly and quickly, condensing the story into as few words as possible, deliberately omitting their own situation.

Alva listened soberly, without interruption, but showed she wasn't deceived. 'If they wreck the oil rig they can't let us go, can they?' she asked steadily.

'No.' Carrick looked at her wrists. They were tied almost as tight as his own, the only difference being that wire flex had been used instead of nylon. 'But if we get one chance –'

'When, not if –' corrected Clapper Bell then stopped short. The work around them had ended and Page Abbott was crossing over towards them from the shore, his arms cradling the scuba gear they'd left on the beach.

He dumped the load beside the motor fisher's wheelhouse stump then came on. When he reached them, he frowned briefly then glanced at the guard. 'Tie their feet. Get them down on the deck first.'

It was done with a length of cord. By the time the man finished the engines of all three boats were started and running throatily.

'Marge –' Abbott beckoned the woman over from *Starglow*'s cockpit, waited till she'd arrived, then gave her a faint smile. 'Time to say goodbye for a spell. You know what to do – you've got one of Skinner's men, take *Starglow* back to Borland, then do as we planned.' He glanced at Carrick. 'They had to have some kind of boat to get here, and my bet is it'll be moored somewhere off-shore. Spot it if you can and get rid of it.'

'Anything else?' she asked tartly.

'Not for now. Just remember I'm relying on you.' Abbott watched her go back, then turned to where his three captives now lay side-by-side.

'Our turn for goodbyes?' asked Carrick sourly.

The man ignored the sarcasm. 'You know the practicalities,' he said almost mildly. 'There's a little time yet – till after we're done, at any rate.' Swiftly, he turned on his heel and left.

The *Anna B.* was first to sail, Skinner Jones at her helm, Abbott and two of the drifter's crew aboard. Next the old motor fisher edged clear, her ancient engine spluttering a little and a thick cloud rising from her exhaust stack. Another of the *Anna B.*'s men was at her controls while Swanson squatted on the deck nearby with the shotgun on his lap.

As the two fishing boats began to head south *Starglow* got under way. Running without lights like the rest, the faint moonlight filtering through the gathering clouds showed her bow swing slowly north. Then her power opened up a few notches, white phosphorescence danced in her quickly gathering wake, and she had gone.

Their engines keeping a steady ten knots, the tidal current from astern building the pace, the two fishing boats travelled on through the night. Occasionally, a stray wavecrest broke over the motor fisher's bow and drenched its curtain of spindrift over the decks. Now and again, a faint splash from the sea around told of some fish making a final, desperate effort to escape a larger predator.

A white flash of light far ahead was the first sign they'd reached the start of the Camas Dubh channel. As the flash was repeated and became a regular part of the skyline, Carrick strained for the hundredth time against his bonds and failed to do anything except cause a fresh agony in his wrists. Yet down there on Whip Light, Jumbo Wills would probably be watching late-night television while Alva's father and the rest of the lighthouse team went through the peaceful routine of their tasks.

The man at the motor fisher's helm grunted something above the beat of the engine. They saw Swanson rise to his feet and, still carrying the shotgun, go back to take his place. Thigh-length fisherman's boots flapping, the *Anna B.*'s deckhand walked towards the bow, passing them without breaking his pace. He reached the bow, bent over a large canvas-wrapped bundle, felt its lashings, then began to return. He slowed this time as he reached them, fumbled in his overall pockets, and put a cigarette in his mouth. Next moment a match flared between his cupped hands. Carrick had a brief glimpse of worried eyes flickering down to meet his own. He'd just recognized the lined face – the deckhand he'd last seen during that scuffle with Skinner Jones – when the match went out and the man strode back to the stern. Swanson nodded briefly and took up his post as before.

Another five minutes passed, the *Anna B.* still a mere hundred yards or so ahead, both boats beginning to roll a little and ship more spray as the swell's pattern was broken by the unseen shoal rock. Suddenly, their helmsman spoke again. For a second time Swanson took over while the fisherman walked the swaying deck to the bow. Again the same bundle was checked and the man began returning. He stumbled a little as the boat rolled and spray drenched the deck, swore, steadied himself, then slipped and almost fell as the return roll began. One hand brushed against Carrick's side while fresh spray pattered around.

Then the man had picked himself up and was heading rapidly aft – while Carrick, wondering if he could be dreaming, felt cold steel against his wrists and a moment later had the cork hilt of his diving knife tight between his fingers.

Neither Clapper nor Alva seemed to have noticed. Slowly, carefully, he worked the knife blade round. But as he felt the honed steel edge make its first contact with the nylon line round his wrists the motor fisher's engine beat slowed.

Ahead, the *Anna B.* had stopped. And swaying in the water beside the drifter was the round shape of the blacklight buoy crowned by the black silhouette of the racon reflector.

Chapter Eight

Moving at a crawl, handled skilfully, the motor fisher edged in until the two vessels formed a V, bow to bow, fenders out, moored to the bulk of the buoy between them. Abbott's voice rapped orders as, his prisoners temporarily ignored, he marshalled the *Anna B.*'s crew to their task.

Straining his neck, Clapper Bell rumbled a grudging approval. 'They've got it well taped, I'll give 'em that much, sir.'

'So far.' Webb Carrick clenched his teeth, muscles protesting as he forced his fingers and wrists to a strained, unnatural angle which still only provided minimum purchase on the knife. He sawed again at the nylon line, saw the bo'sun's eyes suddenly widen with realization and threw him a quick, warning glance. At least one of the *Anna B.*'s men was within easy earshot. Resting a moment, he raised himself a little higher on his elbows and looked beyond Bell. 'Still all right, Alva?'

The girl twisted round on her side and nodded. 'It's hardly comfortable, but –' she shrugged, then looked again at the activity. 'Webb, can it – will that beacon really work like they say?'

'Probably.' He glanced at the bo'sun, signalled in brief, pantomime style with his head, saw Clapper turn towards her, and heard the Glasgow-Irishman's soft whisper. Alva's eyes lit with a quick, eager hope. Then, very deliberately, she looked away.

The operation around them was moving quickly under the pinprick glow of shielded torches. Swanson had taken a small toolkit and was crouched on the hump of the buoy, working with a swift sureness as he unscrewed a small inspection hatch on top. The other men swarmed briefly aboard the motor fisher, unlashed the canvas bundle at her bow, and began dragging loose length after length of lightweight, strangely shaped material. It unfolded like cloth yet seemed awkward to handle, and the torch-beams glinted on the plastifoam coating one side of each section.

Page Abbott planned to put a hood over the racon beacon – a hood already tailored to fit.

The line round his wrists came loose, and Carrick fought down a gasp as the knife blade sliced flesh. He felt a warm trickle of blood, the cork handle became instantly slippery, and for a heart-stopping moment almost escaped his grip. Fingernails digging desperately, he twisted the steel edge round with an infinite care and made contact with the lashing still holding his thumbs. He raised himself up a fraction to gain a better position, then sank back quickly to the deck as Abbott boarded the motor fisher from the buoy and came briskly towards them.

'Not long now, Carrick.' He thumbed over his shoulder to the racon buoy, where the first sections of plastifoam were already being lashed into position. 'Pretty good, eh?'

'Depends on the viewpoint.' Carrick's face tightened as he fought down the agony of returning circulation in his wrists.

Abbott saw the expression, but misunderstood. 'Don't think I'm going to enjoy what's necessary as far as you're concerned,' he said almost regretfully. 'It just has to be, that's all.'

'But you don't even know the *Sea Raven* will show up,' protested Alva, making a deliberate effort to distract the man's attention. 'What happens if there's no sign of it before dawn? All of this is wasted –'

'Sorry.' Abbott regarded her tolerantly but shook his head. 'We know the tow is running on schedule. And we rigged a radar scanner on the *Anna B*. – it's already picking up a fringe echo on maximum range. Another hour at most and the rig will be coming up the channel.' He glanced back at Carrick. 'We're knocking out the middle beacon, dummying up about eight hundred yards further east.' His teeth showed briefly in the darkness. 'Swanson reckons that'll give maximum effect with minimum distance.'

Carrick thought of the Camas Dubh chart, the way the unseen channel swept like a giant dogleg between the shoal rocks, and nodded grimly.

But Alva hadn't finished. She tried again. 'And who gains?'

Abbott shrugged. 'Several people – though some of them won't know why. The Nanda Group's concessions happen to border where one of the major companies has already struck gas – though like big fellows usually do they're keeping quiet and drilling on, because they're ninety-nine per cent certain there's oil lower down. Nanda don't know that yet – and they happen to be a family-owned shoestring outfit, mortgaged to the hilt.'

'So if they lose the oil rig –'

'They're finished. Nanda is taken over by – well, an investment group who already hold a debenture note on its assets.'

Carrick glared up at the man. 'A group you and your friends just happen to have a big interest in, of course?'

'Of course.' Abbott chuckled briefly. 'And you can guess the rest. The moment word gets out about what's next door to the Nanda concession share prices will rocket.'

'Ruddy bandits,' growled Clapper Bell.

Abbott grinned and turned away. A moment later, he was supervising the placing of the final sections of the racon buoy's plastifoam hood. There was no one else near them, and Clapper Bell took his chance.

'How's it comin', sir?' he demanded hoarsely.

'Nearly there,' muttered Carrick. The line round his thumbs was proving even more difficult than his wrists, and the blood still seeping down from the gash above didn't help. He sawed again, felt a sudden release of the binding pressure, and sighed thankfully. 'That's it, Clapper – but we'll pick our time.'

'Aye.' Bell rolled over on his side and told Alva while Carrick again experienced the agonizing luxury of returning circulation. Then, after a moment, he brought his feet up under his body and sawed at the cord tying his legs until it was held by little more than a thread.

'Your turn,' he said quietly. One arm came quickly from behind his back and he pressed the knife's handle into Bell's cupped and waiting hands. As soon as it was done he brought his arm in again and lay still.

He had been just in time. As the knife disappeared behind the bo'sun's burly frame Douglas Swanson clattered back on the motor fisher's deck followed by their helmsman from the *Anna B*. Swanson inspected them perfunctorily then, the shotgun cradled in his arms, stood where he was and regarded the hooded racon buoy with a satisfied air.

The *Anna B*. had cast off. Her engine throbbing quietly, her men aboard, she began to head away to take up position for the main task remaining. As she went, the moonlight pierced briefly through a broken edge of cloud and showed the stark frame of the substitute beacon rising high from near her bow. The motor fisher stayed moored, her car tyre fenders rubbing gently against the buoy with each slow-moving swell.

Swanson watched the other boat go, whistled softly and tunelessly between his teeth for a spell then, as the *Anna B.* finally vanished into the night leaving only the barely discernible sound of her engine, he crossed over and looked at his charges. He grinned, and the shotgun in his hands, held waist-high, lowered until the twin mouths of its barrels were pointed directly at Carrick. For a moment he stared down at Carrick, a taunting amusement in his eyes, then the gun swung on, first to Clapper Bell, then to Alva. In the background, the fisherman by the little wheel-house sat motionless.

At last, still without a word, Swanson grew tired of the game. The shotgun went back under the crook of his arm and he turned to go.

Carrick let him get two paces past, then made his bid. His legs jerked, the last thread of the cord snapped, and he catapulted up and along the deck in a clawing tackle. His weight hit the man squarely behind the knees and they went down together, the shotgun clattering free, Swanson first too surprised to shout then whooping hoarsely as the breath left his lungs under the sheer impact of their fall.

But he recovered fast. A wildly kicking foot took Carrick high in the stomach and for a moment his grip relaxed. Swanson scrambled crab-like in an attempt to reach the shotgun, then Carrick had him again and this time they crashed against the low gunwale. Carrick's right fist smashed into the man's opened mouth, and the small moustache suddenly showed the dark stain of blood. Swanson tried again, his elbow swinging in a short, vicious arc which took Carrick hard on the stomach in an explosion of pain – and for a second time he was diving for the shotgun.

One hand reached the weapon, the gun barrels started to swing in a frantic, clubbing blow, and Carrick threw himself away in a desperate bid to escape. But the blow didn't come. Instead, there was a soft thud, an almost child-like whimper of pain, and, still in a half-crouch, Swanson rocked back and forwards in a mixture of shock and horror. The gun dropped, the arm fell useless at his side, and he stared as if hypnotized at the cork haft of the diving knife protruding from high on his shoulder.

It lasted for a few seconds. Then, as he opened his mouth to scream for help, Clapper Bell, feet still bound together, took one massive hop along the deck. The bo'sun's granite-like head took the man on the point of the chin and Swanson went down like a log, out to the world.

'Had to shut 'im up,' said Bell apologetically, beaming across at Carrick. 'Watch the other one –'

Carrick glanced towards the wheelhouse. The fisherman took a step forward then stopped, uncertain. 'It's over,' Carrick told him. 'Come and lend a hand.'

The man nodded. One hand went into his overalls' pocket and came back out with a clasp-knife. Clapper Bell tensed a fraction as the blade clicked open, but the man came on, stopped, and slashed through the cord binding his ankles.

'Thanks.' Puzzled, still wary, the bo'sun took the knife and went back to free Alva.

'And my thanks too.' Carrick rose slowly to his feet, equally puzzled. 'I saw you yesterday, right?'

'That's right, Chief.' The fisherman spoke hoarsely, then gnawed his lip briefly. 'The name's Harry Johns.'

'And tonight . . .' Carrick left the rest unsaid.

168

The fisherman shrugged uneasily. 'Like I said yesterday, I'm the peaceful type, an' – well, there's a limit. If – if Skinner's daft enough to get tangled up wi' murder then we part company.'

Carrick left him and hurried past Swanson's unconscious figure to the other two. Clapper Bell had cut Alva free and now his massive hands were rubbing life back into her wrists with almost absurdly gentle care. He looked up as Carrick approached, grinned and stopped, rising to his feet.

'I'll get that divin' knife back now.' His head jerked significantly towards Swanson. 'It wasn't his ruddy shoulder I aimed for, but maybe it's jus' as well. Want me to parcel him up?'

'Yes. Then tell our little friend Harry to patch him up.'

'Eh, was it him who –'

'Gave me the knife,' agreed Carrick grimly. 'Conscience, cold feet or both. But watch him.'

As Bell went off, he bent down, put an arm round Alva's waist, and helped her get to her feet. She clung to him for support, grimacing.

'Pins and needles going through me –' She drew a deep breath, the look in her eyes compounded equally of pain and relief. Then she squirmed round, her own discomfort forgotten. 'Webb, what about the beacon?'

'In a minute.' Carrick kept his arm round her slim, supple form and guided her over to the wheelhouse shelter aft. Down the channel the Whip Rock light continued its regular, warning flash. But, though he could have been imagining it, there was what might be a faint glow on the horizon beyond. And by now, a scant yet vital distance to the east, the *Anna B.*'s substitute blacklight beacon must be in position and operative.

His mind raced, trying to grapple with the situation, knowing he'd a limited choice of action yet that within that choice there was still the possibility of disaster. The racon buoy was out of action – and even if there was time, Swanson wasn't likely to help put it back in operation. If they ripped the hood clear the buoy would certainly register as a shape on a radar screen – but the *Anna B.*'s rig would still be the one transmitting the racon signal. And if the drifter was maintaining radar watch Abbott would have an immediate warning something had gone wrong.

'Webb –'

He nodded. 'Alva, could you handle this tub down as far as Whip Rock and warn your father?'

'Yes, but –'

'In a minute.' He rummaged in the wheelhouse locker, hoping to find some kind of flare, a rocket, anything of the type. But it was empty except for a few rags and tools. The last alternative had been removed 'Clapper –'

The bo'sun, his task done, had been watching Harry Johns put a rough bandage on Swanson's shoulder. He grunted and crossed over. 'Sir?'

'Fancy a trip?' He pointed towards the upturned dinghy. 'I thought we might go pay a surprise call.'

'In that thing?' Bell crossed to the little boat, rapped the wood with his knuckles, and was less certain. 'We'd be safer swimmin'.'

'Not against that cross-current.' Still, there was some sense in the suggestion. He looked down at his black rubber scuba suit and decided, 'We'll take the flippers with us and go in on our own the last stretch.'

The bo'sun was happier. 'Fine. Eh . . . this is yours, sir.' He handed Carrick the twin of the diving knife already back in his leg-sheath.

Carrick tucked the knife away, collected the shotgun from the deck, and brought it back to Alva. 'You'd better hang on to this in case Harry decides to change his friends again.'

'I'll manage,' she said soberly. 'But what about you?'

'There's only four of them, they'll be busy – and if we're lucky there may even be another one like Harry among them.' He grinned reassuringly. 'Just give us time to get over then a couple of minutes more for luck. Then cut loose what you can of that hood and get this thing moving for the lighthouse. I'll have a talk with Harry before we go – it won't do any harm to tell him he's still up to his neck in trouble.'

They got the dinghy over the side in record time, hastily muffled the rowlocks with some of the rags from the toolbox locker and a few moments later pushed away from the motor fisher, Alva's low-voiced 'good luck' in their ears.

An oar apiece, they pulled strongly – and Carrick, feeling the cross-current's immediate drag, knew he'd been right not to venture the swim. They eased north a couple of points above where he reckoned the *Anna B.* must be stationed, working in a steady rhythm, the oar blades cutting sweetly into the water, the ancient wood creaking a little under the strain.

It was hard going, slower even than he'd antici-pated, with a growing swirl of water around their feet to underline Clapper Bell's qualms about the dinghy's condition. Once or twice the moon filtered through, and Carrick craned his neck, hoping for some sight of the drifter. But when he did get a bearing, it was from the brief glint of a torch then, seconds later, the quiet throb of her engine.

They rowed a few more yards then shipped the oars and slipped quietly over the stern and, side-by-side, began swimming. The salt water stung like fury against the cut on Carrick's wrist and he swore softly – but this was the easy stage, with the current behind them, carrying them down. By now, he reckoned the

171

big oil rig must be within sight of Whip Rock. It was
going to be close all round, too close for comfort
even if everything went like clockwork. Maybe, after
all, they should simply have cut loose from the buoy
and made a straight dash down to pass on the
warning . . .

The dark shape of the *Anna B.* on ahead pushed the
thought from his head. He signalled to Bell and they
stopped, floating for a moment to be sure of the scene.
The drifter was bow-on to the current, her engine note
steady – Skinner Jones was trying the difficult feat of
compensating for the tidal drag, making a bid to hold
a steady position without putting down an anchor.
That made sense with the *Anna B.*'s need to move fast
once its role was over and the oil rig had been lured
into danger.

Bell edged closer. 'Can't take her from the stern,' he
said hoarsely, then spluttered as he swallowed a
mouthful of seawater. 'Not wi' that screw turnin' –
but we could take her one each side, up for'ard.'

Something large, soft, and unseen brushed its way
over Carrick's legs and a yard-wide jellyfish, its long
sting tentacles searching blindly for prey, drifted past.
He was about to nod when there was a stir of activity
aboard the *Anna B.* Vague shapes moved on her deck,
voices carried on the night air, and a signal lamp
flashed briefly and urgently.

'What's on?' asked Clapper Bell, startled.

'Alva – their radar's spotted the hood coming
loose.' Carrick began swimming, beating along in a
fast crawl-stroke, staying on the surface, trusting to
the drifter's engine-noise and the general activity
aboard to cover the sound of their approach.

When they were twenty yards from the drifter's
bow her dinghy began swinging out on the port side.
They dived under, swam till the vessel's hull was a
dark mass just ahead, then surfaced to starboard. That

side of her deck was deserted, but it took precious seconds to work along to one of the rope-secured car tyre fenders then haul themselves silently aboard and crouch low.

They were just aft of the wheelhouse. The faint glow from the compass binnacle showed Skinner Jones hunched at the helm, the door behind him open and swinging with each slow roll of the hull. A few feet nearer the bow, on the port side, where the dinghy had been lowered, another man stared out in the direction of the buoy. That left two more unaccounted, one of them Abbott – but Carrick hadn't time to complete inventories.

Reaching down, he freed the swim flippers from his feet, waited until Clapper Bell had followed the example, then tapped himself on the chest and pointed to the wheelhouse. Bell nodded, rubbed his hands, and began easing forward towards the other man.

At which moment the absent member of the *Anna B.*'s crew popped up, Jack-in-the-Box style, from the stern hatchway. The man's eyes widened, showed white in the gloom, and he gave a bellow of warning.

Skinner Jones spun round at the same moment as Carrick plunged into the wheelhouse. They collided, grappled, and one of the windows shattered as the *Anna B.*'s skipper lurched back against it. He swore savagely, came back like a bull, and the sheer impetus of his rush carried them both out on to the open deck.

Clapper Bell and the two fishermen were in a furious tangle of arms, legs and flailing fists near the stern hatchway. That much registered with Carrick before he blocked a wild, clubbing blow from his snarling opponent and returned a pistoning, short-arm jab which took Jones low in the ribs. The man floundered back, there was the brief clatter of metal and the

173

binnacle light's glow glinted on the heavy, chromed steel pipe wrench he now held in his right hand.

The man came on, his mouth half-open in a slobbering grin. Carrick's fingers dropped for the hilt of the diving knife but met only the empty sheath – somewhere along the way the knife had vanished. And he'd no time to curse the fact. The pipe wrench swung like a silver streak for his head and he threw himself to one side.

He'd forgotten the hatch. The back of his legs struck the raised edge and next moment Carrick was tumbling. He hit the deck, saw the steel wrench swinging again, and tried to roll clear. The blow glanced down his side, bringing a sudden, rainbow-hued moment of pain before the metal's main force was expended in a hammer-like thud against the planking. Still rolling, he had a dazed, momentary impression of someone else moving behind the drifter skipper then heard a loud cry and a splash from near the bow.

Skinner Jones was coming in again. On hands and knees, the pain in his side still sickening, Carrick watched for the man's arm, gathered every atom of strength that remained and, as the pipe wrench rose, threw himself forward. His one hand gripped the man's wrist, stopping the threatened blow. The other came up in a flat-palmed wrestling move to smack home under the man's chin, pressing up and back. Jones flailed wildly, swinging him round and round, always nearer the stern, trying every way he could to shake loose from the terrible pressure pushing his head still further back.

They fell, the pipe wrench flying from Skinner Jones' grip. He tore himself free from Carrick's grip, staggered upright, then lurched as the *Anna B.* rolled. Still picking himself up, Carrick saw, almost in slow motion, the way the man crashed against the low stern combing, the mad flutter of arms as he tried to retain balance, then the way he disappeared backwards. There was a splash, a scream, and for a fraction of a second the drifter's slow-turning screw seemed to hesitate before it vibrated on.

A heavy footstep on the deck brought him round in a fighting crouch, but it was Clapper Bell.

'Aye, I saw,' said the bo'sun, panting a little for breath, one side of his diving rubbers ripped open from throat to midriff to expose a vast expanse of heaving, hairy chest. 'My two are a' right – one o' them's in the water, holdin' on for life to a fender, an' the other's lyin' up at the bow.'

'There's Abbott –'

'He's away I think,' murmured Bell almost apologetically. 'I was a bit busy, but I saw that dinghy beltin' away a minute or so back.' He took another step nearer the stern, stopped, and shook his head. 'Waste o' time lookin' for old Skinner. You all right, sir?'

'I feel like a horse kicked me.' Carrick winced as he stretched upright, but forced himself towards the wheelhouse. He stopped at the door, and his sigh had nothing to do with the pain in his side. The drifter's radio transmitter had been smashed.

'Looks like Abbott didn't want us usin' it once he'd gone,' mused Bell, coming up behind him. 'Funny he didn't stay an' use that gun. It could have made things awkward.'

'He was more interested in getting clear,' said Carrick grimly. 'Abbott's kind know when their luck starts running out – and they cut their losses.'

He thought hopefully of Alva, now probably well down the channel in the old motor fisher. She should make it all right, but there was still one thing remaining to be done.

'Clapper –' he leaned back against the doorway, savouring the brief respite – 'if that crewman is still holding on better yank him aboard. Then get a

175

hammer, any damned thing, but smash that racon unit up front.'

Bell nodded and hurried forward. Almost automatically, Carrick found the control panel and switched on the drifter's navigation lights. The throb of the engine beneath his feet and the twitching steering wheel reminded him of his next task. He checked the compass, saw they'd swung almost full circle in the last hectic minutes, and gradually brought the *Anna B.*'s bow round towards the east. As the first pounding blow of metal on metal sounded from for'ard he located the searchlight control, switched on the roof-mounted beam, then operated the hand swivel just above his head.

The stabbing beam showed only empty water. Then, suddenly, he let the light click out again, wondering if his eyes were playing tricks. But Clapper Bell was shouting from the bow, the flecks of light he'd thought imagination were navigation lights, and the sound of a throbbing boat engine reached his ears as he almost ran from the wheelhouse to join the bo'sun.

Three minutes later the sleek shape of the *Blue Vine* came alongside, a stocking-capped Jenkins Batford grinning from ear to ear at her helm, every deck light blazing. As the two fishing boats touched, Carrick saw someone else at Batford's side – slim, red-haired, the anxiety in her face vanishing as she saw Carrick and Clapper Bell catch the lines tossed across and secure the two vessels side by side.

Alva Leslie beat the *Blue Vine*'s skipper aboard by a short head, hugged them both, and seemed on the brink of either laughing or crying.

'I – I met him halfway down, Webb. It's all right. Jenkins radioed, the *Sea Raven*'s tow won't come through –'

'Aye, an' we'd have been a bit sooner, only we caught something a bit unusual on the way,' mumbled Batford. He thumbed cheerfully towards a tangled bundle of nets lying on the *Blue Vine*'s usually immaculate foredeck, with the drifter's young engineer, grim-faced, standing guard. 'A wee man in a rowin' boat started bangin' at us wi' a gun, till we dropped that lot on him. Your Mr Abbott's as full o' water as a half-drowned rat, but he'll live.' He seemed to read what was on Carrick's mind. 'Ah, don't worry about young Davey there – since the lassie came on board he's told me a thing or two, and I suppose we'll have more company along soon.'

Carrick nodded understanding and agreement. 'That's how it goes, Jenkins,' he said slowly. 'But I won't forget – Captain Shannon won't either.' He looked along their own deck. 'We've two more for the collection, but Skinner Jones went over.'

'Eh?' Batford frowned. 'Maybe we –'

'Over the stern, Jenkins, while she was under way.'

'Like that.' Batford's face tightened briefly, then he shrugged. 'Well, a man has to pay in different ways – I've heard that said before. Like Harry Johns, now – I left one o' my lads wi' him on the motor fisher, and they'll head back for Loch Rachan.' He looked down to the south, half-expectantly, and this time his grin was a trifle wry. 'There's a ship comin' up, fast. I reckon you'll have more company soon, Mr Carrick. But I've a bottle in my wheelhouse an' you two look like you could use a good dram apiece while you're waiting.'

They followed him aboard, and Carrick didn't bother to glance towards the bundle of nets. Page Abbott could keep for a spell. But there was one question he had to ask.

'Jenkins, didn't you – ah – collect anything else tonight?'

177

The *Blue Vine*'s skipper rubbed a slow hand across his chin. 'Maybe, Mr Carrick. But I'll keep my answer for that old devil Shannon.'

H.M. fishery cruiser *Marlin*, Captain Shannon on the bridge, her big twenty-one inch searchlight pinning the two drifters in its dazzling beam like two vagrant moths, came up on the scene in cavalry-charge style, slowed when a bare three hundred yards away and circled.

'*Blue Vine* –' Shannon's voice came like thunder over the electric loud-hailer – 'I'm coming aboard.'

He did, the *Marlin*'s launch delivering him alongside, Jenkins Batford waiting with a helping hand as he scrambled up on to the deck.

'Nice to see you, captain,' murmured Batford. 'Better late than never, eh?'

Shannon growled from the depths of his beard, glanced round, and gave a brief, satisfied nod as he saw Carrick and Clapper Bell. 'Everything under control, mister?'

'Pretty well, sir,' agreed Carrick.

'Good.' Shannon crossed over, looked them both up and down, and sniffed a little as he caught the liquor fumes on his bo'sun's breath. But, though Clapper Bell stiffened, expecting the worst, the fiery little figure turned instead to Alva. 'And – ah – you, miss?'

'All right now, captain.' She smiled, and Shannon softened a little.

'Well, young woman, you caused some worry – but in a good cause.' He growled into his beard again, vaguely embarrassed. 'I've already had your father on R.T., asking what it's all about. But maybe I'll leave that to you to answer personally.' What he obviously considered the necessary courtesies over, Shannon once more became his aggressive self.

'Now, Mister Carrick, what's the situation?'

Carrick told him, and as he finished the Superintendent of Fisheries gave a grunt of satisfaction. 'Right. Bo'sun –'

'Sir?'

'Fetch me this man Abbott.' As Clapper Bell headed off, Shannon turned his gaze on Jenkins Batford. 'Now you, Batford. You've covered quite a distance tonight, haven't you? Up to Knapp Point, then just about every point in the compass before you sneaked over here.'

'Sneaked, captain?' Batford stroked his long, thin chin with apparent concern. 'Och, a wee bit uncertain, maybe – but that's all.'

'Including that time you were stopped lower down the channel, near Whip Light?' Shannon stood with his feet wide apart, arms akimbo. 'Well, where is it?'

'Now, and how did you know, Captain Shannon?' The *Blue Vine*'s skipper portrayed innocent surprise. 'Here am I just telling the lads a while back that finding that funny wee torpedo tonight is the strangest thing, and –'

'Batford!' Shannon's voice quivered, but he kept control. 'We've proof you sent that letter to the Flag Officer, Scotland. We know you went out to collect that torpedo this evening –'

'Och, now, I think you'd be wise to have a talk with me about this before you go jumping to conclusions –' Batford's voice was soothing, yet strangely confident. But before Shannon's blood pressure could go higher, there were footsteps on the deck and Clapper Bell returned, pushing Page Abbott before him.

Clothing sodden, his sparse hair half over his eyes, shivering, *Starglow*'s thin, pale-faced owner allowed himself to be brought to a halt before them. He saw Carrick, and his eyes blazed something close to hate for a moment. Then a fit of coughing seized him.

179

'Eh, there's maybe a bit too much sea still inside him, captain,' murmured Batford.

Shannon grunted. 'You did that much, at any rate, Batford. You –' one short, stubby forefinger prodded Abbott in the ribs as the coughing stopped – 'are you listening? If it had been left to me, I might not have bothered pulling your miserable carcass aboard.' He regarded the man with a cold disgust. 'They had a good way of dealing with wreckers in the old days, at the end of a rope. But now – well, at least you won't bother anyone for a long spell ahead.'

Abbott shrugged, but said nothing.

'Mister Carrick –' Shannon spun on his heel – 'what's left to be done from your view of things?'

'The Harding woman's on *Starglow*, with one of Skinner Jones' men. They'll be back in Loch Rachan by now.'

Shannon grunted. 'We can radio and ask Neilson to collect them – time the C.I.D. earned their keep. Anything else?'

Slowly, Carrick nodded. 'Yes, sir. But how we do it rather depends on Abbott.'

'More of them, eh?' Shannon's glare raked across their soaked, unhappy prisoner. 'Well, are you going to be helpful?'

The man's mouth twisted wearily, sardonically. 'Do I look that kind of a fool?'

'What you look like to me I wouldn't say in company,' grated Shannon. 'All right, Mister Carrick, let's tidy up here. Batford, I'll take these assorted prisoners off your hands and put three men aboard the *Anna B.* Where's this damned torpedo?'

'In the fish hold, but –'

'We'll leave it there, and I'll put another three men aboard this boat to make sure there's no nonsense. Between them they can collect that motor fisher – but you come back with us, on *Marlin*.'

Unperturbed, Batford scratched his nose with one forefinger. 'It'll be a nice change, captain. And it'll give us a chance o' a talk, eh?'

Marlin got under way the moment her passengers were aboard – and before long, as she headed north for Loch Rachan, her radio operator was handling a stream of outgoing and incoming signals. He worked on, cursing his luck, telling anyone who'd time to listen that he rated himself the most overworked, underpaid character on the entire west coast.

Washed, changed, a broad strip of elastic tape secured firmly round his lower ribs to ease their continued ache, Carrick went up to find Alva Leslie already on the bridge. The redhead was wrapped snugly in Shannon's best duffel coat, and was showing a wide-awake interest in everything around. Somehow, she was even succeeding in drawing a smiling, animated flow of small-talk from the usually taciturn Pettigrew, who'd taken over the watch.

Chuckling, he went below to the wardroom. A seaman was on guard outside the door. Within, Clapper Bell, back in his usual uniform, stood watchfully over Abbott.

'How's our guest, Clapper?'

The bo'sun gave a faint grin. 'Captain Shannon's had a session wi' him, sir. But Mr Abbott still doesn't seem inclined to help.'

'At least he's dried out a bit.' The slop-chest had yielded an old sweater and a pair of torn, oil-stained slacks for Abbott, both several sizes too large. Carrick looked down at him. 'Why not change your mind and save yourself more trouble, Abbott? You know what we want.'

A pair of cynical eyes met his own. 'I can guess. A name – like who killed Nathan Broom. But not from me, and there's no use trying Swanson or Marge. They don't know.'

181

'Which leaves you in an unhappy situation,' mused Carrick. 'I'd say you're number one candidate.'

'Prove it,' invited Abbott. 'Just try and prove it – you can't.'

Carrick shrugged and left him. Halfway along the companionway to Captain Shannon's day cabin he passed Jenkins Batford, coming from that direction. The drifter skipper winked but didn't stop.

Shannon had his cabin door open and was standing scowling by his desk. As Carrick entered, he looked up, sighed, and suddenly seemed a little older, a little more frustrated than usual.

'Well, mister?'

'I looked in on Abbott, sir.' Carrick decided against mentioning Shannon's last visitor. 'He's stubborn.'

Shannon gave a shrug. 'Did he give you that line about Swanson and the woman knowing nothing about the killing?'

'He did,' agreed Carrick thoughtfully. 'But there's time to find out – and to arrange accordingly.'

Grimly, Shannon nodded. 'Then let's get on with it, mister – let's get on with it.'

At four a.m., *Marlin* had arrived in Loch Rachan, quietly moored off the jetty, and a busy, yet quietly unobtrusive traffic had begun between ship and shore. Within an hour the two drifters and the old motor fisher had also sailed in and were moored alongside. But it was almost dawn, before, ready at last, Captain Shannon and Carrick went ashore.

Detective Superintendent Neilson was waiting on the jetty and greeted them with a brief nod – they'd seen him more than once aboard the fishery cruiser in the past few hours.

'All ready this end.' Neilson's eyes were weary, but his voice was grimly hopeful. 'Let's hope this comes off.'

'What about the Harding woman?' queried Shannon.

'No change – just like Swanson. Either they're cast-iron liars or they genuinely don't know what happened to Broom.' He shrugged. 'Probably they can guess, but that's no help.'

When they reached it, the Dairg Tower hotel was still quiet, its guests sleeping, no doubt dreaming of the massive catches they hoped to achieve that day. But the entrance hallway was a blaze of light, and there was a uniformed constable on duty just inside the doorway.

Neilson led a firm, purposeful way across the hallway, past the reception desk, then stopped just short of the cashier's office.

'We put him in here,' he explained. 'It's more convenient than his own place.'

They went in. Sergeant MacNaught was over by the window, a cigarette dangling from his lips. Constable Gregor, suitably wooden-faced, stood a few feet away. But the man who mattered was exploding up from the chair placed between them.

'At last!' Peter Mack's high-pitched voice quivered with indignation. For once, the hotelier wasn't in his kilt – but the dark blue business suit which took its place only served to accentuate the fat little man's unshaven pallor. 'First I get dragged from my bed without an explanation, then I'm kept here for hours like some kind of a criminal –'

'We'd things to do, Mr Mack,' said Neilson icily. He jerked his head towards the window. 'You've seen what's out there, in the loch?'

'He looked a few times,' said MacNaught softly.

'There was nothing else to do,' snapped Mack. 'But all I've seen is darkness and a few boats coming in.'

'They're why you're here,' nodded Neilson, crossing over and perching himself on the desk. His legs swung gently. 'It's covered by that old phrase "helping with inquiries".'

'Well –' the hotelier hesitated, then pursed his lips – 'if I can, I will. It's about Broom's death again, I suppose?'

'Partly.' Neilson studiously ignored him for a moment, lighting a cigarette. The others took their cue from him and stayed silent, motionless. He took a long draw on the cigarette and let the smoke trickle slowly. 'The rest is Page Abbott.'

Mack showed not a muscle-twitch of emotion. 'Abbot? Yes, I know him – only as a guest, of course.'

'You're sure?' Neilson's voice chilled a few more degrees. 'Because here's another little tit-bit for you, Mr Mack. He's under arrest – and the *Sea Raven* won't come through the Camas Dubh channel till daybreak.'

'That's supposed to mean something to me?' Mack lowered himself back into the chair and looked around him, his voice tightly precise. 'I don't understand, I'm sorry.'

'All right.' Neilson gave a long sigh. 'Carrick, you tell him.'

'You've caused a lot of people to work hard tonight, Mr Mack,' said Carrick grimly. 'Asking questions, checking, making sure – all in the last few hours. But they've come up with the answers. Like a firm called Wiltra Investments. You know them?'

A flush began to creep over Mack's plump, round face and spread upwards until it covered the bald scalp above. He nodded.

'Abbott runs that company with a dummy front of directors and a parcel of borrowed money, a lot of it borrowed from you. And you decided you'd like a bigger return – especially as you'd mortgaged this place to the hilt in the process.' He stopped for a moment. Shannon was leaning against the wall, frowning, hands deep in his jacket pockets. The three policemen were silent, attentive, their eyes on Mack. 'You've known him a long time, haven't you?'

184

'Yes.' It came grudgingly. 'But –'

Carrick cut him short. 'You served together for a spell during the war, didn't you? "Served" is the word, I think – two years in detention for syphoning army stores into the Cairo black market, wasn't it?' He didn't wait for an answer. 'But this was a whole lot bigger –'

'Whatever it is, I'm not involved ...' The man squirmed in his chair, composure vanishing. 'All right, the rest is true, but whatever Abbott may be saying –'

'He's saying nothing,' rumbled Captain Shannon, stirring from his post. 'But don't let that light any happiness for you, mister – we don't need him.'

'Because we've got enough on our own.' Carrick walked quietly to the window and looked out at the gradually lightening sky. 'My guess is only Abbott and Skinner Jones knew you were involved. Exactly how much Skinner was told – well, that's another thing. He's dead.' He swung round, and saw the man moistening his lips. 'Want me to go through the catalogue, all the little things that add up now?'

'I'll tell him a few,' volunteered Neilson, laying aside his cigarette. 'Like how he forced through a change of date for the fishing festival for "accommodation reasons" – the same week *Sea Raven*'s completion and sailing date was announced. Or how Abbott's entry was squeezed in after the competition list was officially closed.' He saw Mack's startled glance and nodded. 'Jean MacDonald dug that one up. And – well, Sergeant MacNaught and I did a little digging on our own at Campbeltown airport yesterday evening. Abbott was there on Sunday, collecting an air freight package – radio spares, addressed to you. I can guess what kind of spares they'll be when they're traced back.' He shrugged. 'We wondered about the extra mileage on Broom's car. It looks like

185

he followed Abbott down there, knowing a little, guessing a lot – it's just a pity that he didn't know who that package was addressed to – or that he didn't tell us what he'd found out.'

'Aye,' growled Sergeant MacNaught. 'If he had, he'd still be alive.'

Mack was breathing heavily, as if he'd just finished a long, hard run. His hands gripped the arms of the chair, knuckle-white. 'I've a right to see a lawyer –'

'Naturally,' agreed Neilson calmly. 'Once we've finished – and you'll need him.' He slid down from the table, took two long strides which brought him towering over the hotelier. 'Who killed him, Mack?'

'Not me.' Mack shook his head violently. 'Maybe Abbott – I don't know.'

'Even Abbott didn't try that one.' Carrick came over to Neilson's side, staring down at the man with a new disgust. 'Swanson and Marge Harding don't know much, but they do know where Abbott was when Broom was killed – and that's out in the motor fisher, running tests with their racon marker down in the Camas Dubh channel. They were there, Mack – because we picked up their signals, without knowing what was going on.'

'And don't blame a dead man,' rumbled Shannon. 'Skinner Jones wouldn't tie a knot like that fankle round Broom's waist.'

'Which leaves just you,' murmured Neilson. 'Carrick had an idea we should check some of the storerooms behind the hotel for the place Alva Leslie was kept before she was shipped out on the *Anna B*. We did – and we found a sack, with a few red hairs sticking to it. There was a bonus beside it, a length of rope. You know what a microscope can do with that rope, comparing it with the one we found on Broom? Maybe we'll put the same microscope to work on that little stocking knife you're so fond of wearing with that kilt – check the blade edge against the cut end of that nylon fishing line? It can be done, man – I'll guarantee it.' He didn't bother to add that, when it came to the line, he'd be less likely to guarantee the possible result.

'Well –' Mack swallowed before he could bring himself to go on – 'there's not much left, is there?'

'Not much, except why?' said Captain Shannon soberly. 'What was it – did he come and ask for help?'

For almost a minute Mack sat immobile, while the men around could sense him struggling against accepting the inevitable. At last, he shrugged. 'That was it. Broom had been watching *Starglow*. He – he made one check and decided it was empty, tried again later, and was scared off by the girl.' Having begun, he seemed to find talking a relief. 'He came back here. I was at the reception desk – I always do a late stint on Sundays because of the bar trade. He hung around, then wanted to use the phone to call the police.'

'But you found out why and talked him out of it?' suggested Neilson softly.

'More or less.' Mack gnawed on his lower lip. 'I told him I'd fetch the village constable, but then I sold him the idea that Abbott might be already looking for him if the girl had passed the word. Broom didn't take much persuading – he was frightened by then. So, well, I told him to wait along the shore, that he could make as if he was doing some night-fishing from the beach and if anyone saw him they'd pay no attention.'

'Then you went out after him – alone.' Carrick's mouth tightened as he pictured the rest. 'What was the worst part, Mack? Killing him – or moving him around afterwards, having to get rid of his luggage and the car?'

'The worst part?' Weary now, vaguely defiant in a way which was almost grotesque, Peter Mack forced a laugh. 'We'd have cleared a minimum of three hundred thousand pounds on this. More money than you'd earn in a dozen lifetimes, Carrick – and it's gone.'

'Don't cry on my shoulder,' said Superintendent Neilson bluntly. He reached for another cigarette, changed his mind, and instead glanced significantly at Shannon and Carrick. 'Time for the caution and charge routine, Captain Shannon – I'd prefer if we did it on our own.'

Shannon gave a curt nod of understanding, beckoned to Carrick, and the two Fishery Protection men headed for the door. It closed behind them, cutting off the sound of Neilson's new, coldly formal beginning.

'That's it, finished as far as we're concerned,' said Shannon with a brusque thankfulness. Then, as they headed across the hallway, he slowed again, frowning, at the sight of Clapper Bell waiting patiently beside the constable at the exit door.

'Signal for you, sir.' The bo'sun handed over a small buff message envelope, his face expressionless. But as the Superintendent of Fisheries ripped it open and glanced at the message form his right eyelid quivered a fractional wink in Carrick's direction. 'Eh – any reply, sir?'

'No.' Shannon stared down at the message form and swore under his breath in a way which held a tinge of admiration. 'Where is he, bo'sun?'

'Outside, sir. Will I – well, bring him in, sir?'

Shannon looked up quickly, his eyes narrowed. But Clapper Bell's face was still innocently wooden. 'Get rid of him, bo'sun – just get rid of him.'

'Aye aye, sir.' Bell saluted quickly and hurried out. There was a certain, fine-gauge air about *Marlin*'s captain which threatened storm cones ahead.

Carrick waited a moment longer then cleared his throat. 'Batford and his torpedo, sir?'

188

'Correct.' Shannon chewed bitterly on his beard. 'Mister, I'd have staked my first year's pension that we had him. But not now – not this time.' The message form crumpled into a ball beneath his fingers and he thrust it into one pocket.

'Sir?' Carrick raised a cautious eyebrow.

'He took precautions, Mister Carrick.' The words came out like angry wasps. 'We can prove he had a letter posted to naval headquarters – but we can't prove what was in it. He spun me a story tonight, and I signalled Flag Officer Scotland, for confirmation.' Shoulders hunched, Shannon drew a deep breath. 'Well, now I've got it. They've a letter on file from one Jenkins Batford, posted from Glasgow on Tuesday – properly signed, properly addressed, about another damned thing altogether.'

Carrick whistled and was rewarded with a glare. 'Two letters?'

'We know it, he knows it,' grated Shannon. 'He gives one letter to a fellow he's pretty certain we're likely to trace if things narrow down to the *Blue Vine*. But the other –' he shook his head at the futility of the notion – 'dammit, we could search till hell freezes and probably never know who handled it.'

'So now, sir?'

'Now?' That was the last straw as far as Shannon was concerned. 'Flag Officer Scotland wishes official thanks and congratulations extended to one Skipper Batford for retrieving their torpedo. And Skipper Batford's application for a commission in the Royal Naval Volunteer Reserve as received will receive full and prompt consideration.'

He swore again and went stumping out of the building, leaving Carrick standing.

Carrick didn't try to follow. His captain, he decided, was best left alone for a spell. Grinning, he took out his cigarettes, lit one, and stuck his hat a little further back on his forehead.

It seemed a long time since he'd had more than a few hours' sleep, but maybe he'd passed the stage of feeling tired. Suddenly, he knew what should come next. It was tied up with a red-haired girl, a cove with silver sand, and a stretch of cool, welcoming water.

Mind made up, Carrick headed for the door. Outside, the sun was already rising red over Loch Rachan.